DEAD MAN IN THE HARBOUR

AN EAST COAST PORT MYSTERY

H. PAUL DOUCETTE

ISBN: 978-1-68046-545-7

Melange Books, LLC
White Bear Lake, MN 55110
www.melange-books.com

Published in the United States of America.

Cover Design by Ashley Redbird Designs

For Maureen...my Muse

HISTORICAL NOTES

ACKNOWLEDGMENT

I want to thank the staff at the Halifax Regional Municipal Archives, the Nova Scotia Public Archives, and the Map Department at Dalhousie University for their assistance in my research for this story.

A special thanks to my friend Tim Cohoon for his input and much appreciated review of the story.

PROLOGUE

September 11, 1939

It was Saturday morning and my turn to pull weekend duty. I was sitting at my desk drinking my first cup of coffee of the day, reading the paper. I have been a detective with the Halifax Police Department for over eight years. It was a small department located in the basement of the city hall building on Duke Street. Small and quiet, but then there really wasn't that much serious crime here, not like what I had to deal with when I was on the Boston force.

My name is John Robichaud, Robie to my friends.

I was reading the morning edition of the *Chronicle*, keeping up on the situation in Europe. Today's paper leader read: '*DOMINION AT WAR WITH GERMANY*'

I wasn't surprised. I was expecting this because Britain had declared war days earlier.

"Mornin'," my partner, Pete Duncan, said when he entered the squad room. "Anythin' interestin'?"

I flipped the paper around showing him the front page.

"Guess that's that, then," he said, hanging his overcoat on a peg on the wall. He went and poured a cup of coffee, then raised the pot to me.

I shook my head. "Thanks, I'm good, and yeah, no big surprise. Anyone who didn't think this was comin' had their heads in the sand."

"Or up their arses," Duncan said from his desk.

"Yeah, or that. So? What're you goin' to do?"

We had discussed what he would do if Canada went to war: enlist or stay on the force.

"Don't know. Morrison said that we were bein' classed as exempt from enlisting because we're workin' in one of the essential services."

"I heard. So, that mean you're thinkin' of stayin' on the force?'"

"Yeah, I suppose it does. I'm thinkin' things are about to get a bit innerestin' around here pretty soon. Besides, an old fart like you will need someone to carry the weight."

"Whaddya figure the chances are?" I said with a hint of sarcasm.

In fact, everything did change. Within weeks, the city went from a quiet commercial port to a bustling military port with the influx of war materials, men, and merchant and naval shipping, as the Atlantic convoy system was gearing up. There was also the inevitable increase in illegal enterprises looking to profit from the circumstances, namely, prostitution, bootlegging, gambling, and black marketers. Fortunately for the small 70-plus police in the force in general, much of the policing was shared with the three services, especially in matters of port security. However, events were about to transpire that would draw me and my partner into the world of naval intelligence.

"Anythin' special come in overnight?" Duncan asked.

"Just more of the usual—monitor the local German, Italian communities, like we got that many," I said.

"Guess we should expect more of that sorta stuff these days."

"Yeah, I know. So, what's the latest on that business on Bauer Street?"

"We got the guy. He's a Greek merchantman likes to gamble. Got into a floating game run by our buddy Jacobs. Seems he was losin' too much and accused the dealer of cheatin'. Pulled a knife and cut him up a little. The uniforms managed to deal with most of it. The Greek is in lockup along with a coupla of the others."

"Jacobs?" I asked.

Duncan shook his head.

"Figures. He's almost never at any of the games. What about this dealer? The one who was cut up?"

"Minor injuries, stitches mostly, will be released later today. Want to bring him in?"

"Yeah. Let's talk to him. Maybe he'll give us somethin' we can use."

"Okay. I'll send a uniform over," Duncan said, picking up the phone on his desk. I went back to my paper, thinking that the news would be a lot worse in the days and months ahead.

There had been a marked increase in military activity in and around the port as preparations were underway to bring the harbour defences up to standard. The military also began a steady growth in personnel in the three services based here, anticipating the escalation of hostilities in Europe. Halifax was woefully unprepared both with its port infrastructure and security capabilities, which had declined significantly since the end of World War I. Fortunately, steps to address these issues had begun early in the year.

The British Admiralty recognized the importance that Halifax would play if war was declared and, with the cooperation of the government, took steps. One of the first steps taken was in the area of port defence and security. It was believed that the Abwehr had positioned agents throughout Canada and the United States. Acting on this belief, they installed an intelligence unit in Halifax.

November 1939

It was a clear, moonless night. Off to his right, he could just about make out the silhouette of the net tender; looking seaward, he spotted the intermittent flashes from a signal lamp. A convoy ship approaching, he guessed. Luckily for him, the patrols did not pay too much attention to this side of the anti-submarine nets.

He rowed the small skiff against the incoming tide, struggling to keep the unstable boat from rolling and tossing him out. His arms ached and sweat rolled down the inside of his heavy woolen overcoat, despite the cold wind that blew down the narrow inlet known locally as the Northwest Arm.

Looking over his left shoulder, he spotted the low wooden dock jutting out into the water. He manoeuvered the boat quietly up to it, shipped his oars and grabbed one of the posts. He sat listening in the darkness under the dock. Satisfied, he secured the boat, then took out a small flashlight and, covering the glass end with a hand, turned it on over his watch: two twenty-two.

He was running late. There was only an hour and a half, if he was lucky, before the fishermen started down to their boats, which were anchored at various points along the rocky shore. He had time, he thought, as he stepped out of the boat.

He made it about a hundred feet down the dirt trail leading to a hill under York Redoubt: his final destination. This was a reconnaissance mission to locate the power source for the newly installed searchlights used by the British as part of their port defence system. According to information he received from one of his contacts in the city, the army had built a generator station somewhere in the wooded area below the gun placements.

He made his way to the edge of the wooded area where he found the path that would lead to the site's location. Suddenly, he heard the sound of an on oncoming vehicle from the top of the hill. He quickly stepped off the path and into a clump of trees, pulling his gun from inside his coat.

The vehicle was a three-quarter-ton army truck with six soldiers in the back, all armed with rifles. A staff sergeant sat in the front in the passenger seat.

The truck came to a stop and he got out, ordering the men to dismount.

"Okay, lads. Fan out and keep an eye peeled. The bugger's s'ppose to be in here somewhere," he said, taking his sidearm, a Webley Mk IV .38, out of its holster, and holding up a large torch in the other hand, fanned it slowly across the area.

After a few moments, one of the men shouted out, "Over here."

Cafferty knew he had been set up and that there was no way out. He might get one of them, maybe even two, but they would surely gun him down. He decided to give himself up and take his chances. He liked living.

Letting the pistol hang from a finger, he stepped from behind the tree as the staff sergeant's light landed on him.

"I give up. Don't shoot."

Five hours later, he found himself in a windowless room back in the city, sitting at a small wooden table with two chairs. They had left him a pack of cigarettes, a box of matches and a glass of water. A single stark white light at the end of a corded wire hung from the ceiling over his head. When they brought him in they removed everything from him except for his shirt, pants and socks. So far, no one had spoken to him or threatened him in any way. It wasn't what he expected. He remembered being "'questioned'" by the bastards back in Ireland.

The door opened and a young looking naval officer, a lieutenant, entered carrying two mugs of tea and a file tucked under his arm. He came over and passed one of the mugs across the table, setting it down in front of him. He pulled the other chair closer and sat down.

"My name is Parks," he said, setting his mug down and opening the file. "You are Denny Cafferty, correct?"

Cafferty saw no point in lying or not answering since they obviously knew something.

"Yes," he said, without any rancour.

"You are a member of the IRA, correct?"

"You know that already, so why ask?"

"Just answer the questions," Parks said, looking back at the open file.

"I see that you have been busy back in Ireland."

Cafferty just sat there waiting.

"In fact, we have been advised that Special Branch would like to get their hands on you."

Again, silence.

"Right. Let's get to it, shall we? What were you doing at the Redoubt?"

Parks sat staring at him for several minutes but said nothing.

Cafferty closed the file and leaned forward.

"You are in a very difficult position. We have caught you at a secure military installation under suspicious circumstances to say the least, and armed. We have an arrest-on-sight order from Special Branch with instructions to ship you right back to England where you will face subversion and sabotage charges against the state in time of war. I believe that means a visit to the hangman."

He paused to let it all this sink in, then said, "Your choices seem to have vanished."

"Get to it already," Cafferty said after a moment. "What do you want?"

Parks sat back. "I think you already know the answer to that question."

Parks watched as Cafferty sat considering his fate. He knew they had him. It would be a simple matter to wrap him up and send him back to England, but this was too good an opportunity to get a foothold into any German operation here in Nova Scotia, provided they turned him.

"Right, so what's it to be? Work for us or Special Branch?" Parks asked after a few moments of letting his situation sink in.

"Bastards."

"Is that a yes?"

Cafferty sat sullenly glaring at the young officer as the reality of his position took hold. He knew he was done for and had no other options open to him. He sank back into the chair in resignation.

"Right," Parks said, pulling out a sheet of paper and sliding it with a pen across the table.

"What's this?" Cafferty said, sitting forward.

"The Official Secrets Act. Sign where you see the X."

"Why do I hafta sign this?"

"Let's just say it's additional insurance of your, uh, new loyalties. Also, it means that if you contravene the act, then you will be subject to certain very serious consequences."

"You mean you'll hang me if I don't do what you want."

"Not at all, old chap. We don't hang people in the service. We put you against a wall and face you before six men with rifles and shoot you in the heart," Parks said complacently.

Cafferty swore as he picked up the pen and etched his name on the paper.

He spent the next three days locked away in the basement of the headquarters building being interrogated by a couple of men. By the end of that time he had given up everything he knew about the IRA's operations here, including the names of Sean O'Toole and Iain Kelly. However, he could not provide them with anything sufficient to pick these men up and detain them. He was also pressed for any knowledge of German activities and agents in Halifax. The only thing he could provide was that he heard of an agent being here, but that was all.

Over the next few months, he continued doing what he was sent there to do but under heavy control by the navy. They also used him to pass along false and misleading information cleverly inserted into true, but inconsequential, information.

Unfortunately for him, there was an IRA sympathiser working at the headquarters building.

CHAPTER ONE

March 1940

It was a typical cold, sunless March day, the type of cold you feel deep in the bones from a stiff northerly wind with teeth in it blowing out of Bedford Basin. The sky, a flat ceiling of grey featureless clouds, seemed to press down, adding to the feeling of dreariness.

Sean O'Toole walked along the sidewalk cowering inside his great woolen coat, the collar pulled high up the sides of his face. Up ahead he saw the entrance to the Merchantman's Club, his destination. Moments later, he stood just inside and with a brief involuntary shudder, relaxed and removed his coat. Looking around the room he finally spotted Michael Cavanaugh sitting at a table in the corner. He made his way through several men standing around the table with an urn of coffee on it. He poured a mug, then went to join Cavanaugh.

"What's up?" O'Toole asked as he dropped his coat over the back of the chair and sat down.

"Somethin's come up ya need ta know about," Cavanaugh said, leaning forward.

"Yeah? What's that, then?"

"Yer mate. Cafferty."

"What about him?"

"He was picked up by the navy intelligence guys."

O'Toole leaned in. "You sure? When?"

Cavanaugh nodded, saying, "Yeah, I'm sure. I was standin' right there in da lobby when he came in lookin' all nervous like, you know, lookin' all over the place makin' sure no one seen him. Anyway, he then heads fer the basement an' ya knows what down there."

"When was this?"

"Yesterday," Cavanaugh said, sitting back.

"Jesus Christ," O'Toole cursed.

"I take it dis ain't good."

"No fuckin' shite, it ain't good," O'Toole spat. "Okay. You did real good. We'll remember this."

"Wasn't nuttin'. Jus' doin' my little bit for The Cause, yeah."

"Well, it was more than a little bit this time, buddy. You still safe over there?"

"Yeah. They ain't got no idea I'm wit' you."

"Okay. Thanks for this. For now, you keep at it. If anythin' changes, I'll be in touch somehow."

"Gotcha," Cavanaugh said, finishing his coffee, then standing up. "I better git back."

"Okay, and thanks again." O'Toole shook his hand.

O'Toole sat for a few minutes after Cavanaugh left, drinking his coffee and letting this news sink in.

If Cafferty had been taken and was turned by naval intelligence, then everything the IRA was doing here could be compromised. If he broke, what could he tell them? Himself for sure. Kelly? Maybe. The German? Unlikely. What else could he give up? He had to let the others know right away. He checked his watch: three forty-five. He was meeting the German around four o'clock.

The German had arrived in Halifax in August 1939. His real name was Kurt Klepp. His cover was as Carl Borden travelling to Halifax in search of employment as a riveter. His real mission was to find his way to Halifax and once there establish contact with an IRA man named Iain Kelly who would help set him up with accommodation and work as a cover; that was four months ago. In fact, he did get a job with the railway working in the repair yard on damaged boxcars.

His father was a minor diplomat serving in Washington at the German Embassy in the Trade Department, holding this post for eight years. As a result, he received a good education there. Upon the family's return to Germany in 1928, Klepp entered the military officer academy. When he graduated he enlisted in the Wehrmacht as an Oberleutnant, or lieutenant.

Eight months before Germany invaded Poland and war was declared with Britain, Kurt Klepp found himself sitting outside the office of Oberst von Lahousen at Abwehr headquarters in Berlin along with three other young officers. Von Lahousen was in charge of Abwehr Subdivision II, German Intelligence.

Klepp arrived wearing his dress uniform, his shoulder boards indicating his rank: Oberleutnant. He had answered a general summons for any member of the military with fluency in English to report here for a special interview. By the end of the interview he had been recruited into the Abwehr and sent on an extensive training course. When he finished he was assigned to North American operations, based in New York. Not long after the outbreak of hostilities, he was re-assigned to Canada with orders to proceed to the port city of Halifax where the Allies were staging their convoys to England.

His orders were to gather as much information as he could on troop and material movements, cargoes and convoy activities, as well as port defences, if possible. This would be transmitted to a waiting U-boat that would surface every other night for five minutes at a predetermined set of variable times. His cover was that of a riveter travelling to Halifax in search of employment.

Now, the two men sat at the wooden kitchen table with a pail, two glasses of beer, and a full ashtray on it. The two-room apartment was located on the second floor of a cold-water flat on the north end of

Brunswick Street. It was owned by a local bootlegger who sometimes ran a floating card game out of it. O'Toole knew the man who lived downstairs so was able to get access whenever he needed someplace to meet someone on the sly. He always felt uneasy meeting this man. He didn't even know his name.

The bare forty-watt light hanging from the ceiling on a twisted cord made the room look bleaker than usual. The smells from years of cooking and burning coal hung thick in the room. A small tin pail sat on the table half-full of lukewarm beer.

"Too bad. He could have proved useful over time," Kurt Klepp said casually.

"He's a traitor to The Cause," O'Toole said.

Sean O'Toole came over from the old country about five years ago. He was Irish to the core and an IRA soldier. He had no love for the British, so when he was contacted with an offer to help The Cause by an uncle back home who was an active member of the IRA, he gladly accepted.

His contact, Iain Kelly, called him a while back telling him that an IRA soldier was being sent across, his name Denny Cafferty. He would also be contacted by a German named Kurt Klepp, due to arrive in Halifax soon. He assumed that this Cafferty's assignment was to get and pass information to the German, but that wasn't the case. Seemed Cafferty was a specialist in explosives, which meant sabotage. That was over a year ago.

"Yes, of course, you're right. It was most fortunate that your contact was able to alert you so quickly."

"You know what they say about Irish luck," O'Toole said.

"Hmm, yes. Luck. How much of our operation did he know?"

"Not a lot, I don't think. He wasn't involved with some of our other businesses."

"The weapons and explosives?"

"Safe away."

"Good. I think we had better take precautions, since it's a very good chance that he's told them about us. I think you should call him and arrange a meeting somewhere away from prying eyes and ears, yah?"

"Yeah, okay," he said, getting up and going to the phone. A few minutes later he came back to the table and sat down.

"Done. He'll be down at the docks near midnight. It's dark and we can take care of this outta sight."

"Excellent. I think it may be time for us to consider our other options, don't you think? I mean, if he has talked to the intelligence services, then you are at some risk, yah?"

"Already in the works. If I hafta, I can get outta the city and then up to Boston. You?"

"Better you don't know," Klepp said, checking his watch. "And you are certain he suspects nothing?"

"Yes. Why would he?"

"Good. Let us meet up again at eleven, yah? Then we go together," Klepp said and, standing up, reached for his overcoat.

"Okay. I got some things I hafta take care of anyway."

Klepp left first. O'Toole sat at the table for a few minutes finishing his beer, considering his next move.

He definitely had to warn Kelly of the situation. That was paramount.

Twenty-five minutes later he was at Kelly's place on Inglis Street. Unfortunately, Kelly wasn't there and no one had any idea when he'd return. O'Toole decided to hang around until it was time for his meeting with Klepp, hoping that Kelly would come back before then. He had no idea what he should do about Cafferty, which was why he needed to talk to Kelly. One thing was for sure, he thought as he sat in Kelly's private rooms drinking a hot mug of tea. Cafferty had to be dealt with immediately.

Denny Cafferty was a soldier with the IRA. He was part of an operation called the S-Plan, targeting major cities within Britain with bomb attacks. Unfortunately, his last assignment failed and he barely escaped capture. On the run from the British, he made it back to Ireland. He was smuggled out of Ireland and sent to Canada, landing in Halifax in the fall of 1937. Before leaving he was given a name, Iain Kelly, and an address.

He quickly found out how closed and dull this city was: no pubs, severely restricted access to booze, nothing. Of course, there were the usual dives and rip-off joints found in any seaport, and, of course, plenty of prostitutes. But it was the number of British here that lit the fire in his belly the most. Like Brits everywhere, they were sure to be at the top of order and didn't seem to suffer from the privations the rest of the city suffered. This made working against them even more important, collecting information on the war activities in the port and passing it along to the council back in Ireland. He might be in exile, but doing this would make being away from Ireland tolerable knowing that he was helping to defeat the bastards.

It didn't take Cafferty long to make connections with the city's seedy underbelly He quickly set up a couple of earners to bring in extra cash. It was through these that he was able to obtain the information he needed. He was able to see and report on the defensive developments in the port as well as the increases in shipping traffic.

Unfortunately for him, he was eventually caught by the intelligence service a month ago trying to obtain information about the installation at York Redoubt. He was looking at the possibility of life in prison, a return to England, or even death. However, they offered him an opportunity to work for them and, he decided that his dedication to The Cause only went so far, so he accepted the offer. Now here he was waiting for the man he usually passed the now doctored information to. He knew that he was taking a big risk but he was caught in a bind. His past had caught up to him. One way or the other, he knew he was screwed.

It was a cold moonless night, just the kind of night for making mischief. Cafferty now stood shivering in the deep shadows of the shed at Pier 26 waiting for his contact to show up. He was surprised when O'Toole had called for a meeting. He said there were new instructions from the council he had to pass along. Still, he thought, it was odd.

The waterfront was busy with ships loading and unloading cargoes destined for the war effort. The noise was a pain in the ass, he thought, standing in the dark shadow of the shed at the end of a rail line, but it worked for him. No one would notice him there in the dark, waiting.

He needed a smoke but resisted, not wanting to draw any attention to his position. He was feeling on edge, jumpy.

He checked his watch with the penlight he had...twelve ten.

Suddenly he heard approaching footsteps in the gravel and saw someone approaching from around the end of the boxcar.

Two men stepped out of the shadows. Cafferty recognized one of the men, Sean O'Toole, his IRA contact.

"What's the reason for this meetin'?" Cafferty asked in a hushed voice. "We ain't s'pose to meet for another coupla days."

"We have a problem," O'Toole said, ignoring Cafferty's question.

"Yeah? And what's that?" Cafferty said, sounding irritated.

Suddenly O'Toole moved, quickly grabbing Cafferty from behind, pinning his arms in a firm grip.

"What the hell!" Cafferty said, suddenly overcome with fear as he watched the stranger slowly screw a suppressor onto the pistol he held.

"Ya fucked up, Denny me lad," he said into his ear. "Did ya think we'd not find out?"

"I...I don't know what yer talkin' about," Cafferty said, weakly.

The other man had pulled out his gun. O'Toole watched in horror as he raised it, placed the end of the suppressor against the back of Cafferty's head behind his left ear and slowly squeezed the trigger. He heard the click of the gun's hammer being pulled back then...nothing.

Cafferty's head snapped violently to the side. Blood and bits of his brain had sprayed over Klepp's face, his nostrils filled with the stink of cordite and burnt hair. Seconds later, he felt Cafferty's dead body slide from his grip to the gravelled ground.

"Quick. Grab his feet and help me to the car," Klepp said as he put the gun away.

O'Toole bent down grabbing Cafferty's ankles. They managed to get him back to the car the German drove to the meeting, then stuffed him in the trunk.

"I'll take it from here. You go. I'll contact you later," Klepp said.

Sean O'Toole walked quietly down the dark track to the main road. He was concealed inside the black woolen overcoat he wore, its collar pulled high over his face. He pushed his hands deep inside the overcoat's pockets.

He still felt queasy. It was the first time he had seen a man shot to death up close, that, and the reality of how dangerous a game he was into with the German hit him.

This one was a cold bastard. No humour, no emotion. An Abwehr agent and a dedicated Nazi, a believer, and probably a member of their SS. Mid-twenties, five-nine, athletic build. Not bad looking in an ordinary way, not flashy but enough to appeal to most young women. Unlike a lot of Aryan types associated with the true Nazi, he had a darkish complexion with dark hair and eyes, but O'Toole knew...he was a cold-blooded killer. He could still see him, pistol in his hand placed at the back of Cafferty's head, and then casually squeezing the trigger.

"Jesus, I need a drink," O'Toole muttered as he turned off the road and up onto the tracks that ran into the distant station.

He cut across the rows of track from the docks to Barrington Street, heading for Kelly's place. Rail traffic was busy as usual—cars coming and going, boxcars being shunted around the various sheds. Fortunately, the streets were less busy at this end of the city, except for the foot traffic, as servicemen and seamen went in search of cheap booze and good times. He spotted a half-dozen or so doxies trying to hustle the men who stood outside the bootlegger's place waiting their turn to get in. Across the street, in an alley dimly lit by a streetlight, he could just make out a man leaning against a wall and someone crouching or kneeling in front of him.

Last chance to make a couple of dollars, he thought, looking away.

He moved past a few men, ignoring their gripes, and opened the front door and went inside. Squeezing his way through the crowded hallway followed by a string of muttered curses, he reached the stairwell. The air was thick with smoke and the smell of pressed bodies still wearing heavy coats and uniforms. Somewhere in one of the side rooms, a radio played music.

"Christ. You look like shit," Iain Kelly said when he reached the private room on the second floor.

Iain Kelly was IRA and the head of their operations here in Halifax. He had been here since 1928. He was sent over originally to coordinate with the IRA's operations in the United States, particularly in Boston, mostly handling the transfer of funds and movement of guns but with the outbreak of the war he took on a different role. Only Sean O'Toole knew this.

"Yeah," O'Toole said, unbuttoning his coat.

"Siddown and have a drink." Kelly poured two fingers of Irish whisky into an empty glass and passed it to him. The whisky was from his private stock, not the rotgut he was selling downstairs.

"Heard you were here earlier. What happened?"

Sean downed the drink in a single gulp, coughing slightly at the end from the heat at the back of his throat. He took out a pack of Buckingham's and tapped out a couple of cigarettes, offering one to Kelly, who took it.

"Cafferty," Sean said, flipping open his lighter and holding the flame up.

"Yeah, so?" Kelly said, leaning down slightly and lighting up.

"He's dead."

"Huh? Whaddya mean dead?"

"He was workin' for the Brits. I met him half an hour ago with our other friend. Anyway, he shoots him in the head. Bang. Just like that. Christ almighty, man. I ain't never seen anythin' like that before."

"Jesus. Cafferty workin' with the Brits. I don't believe it. He hated the bastards."

"That might be, but our source at naval headquarters saw him goin' inta the buildin' yesterday. He says he went him straight downstairs. That's where the intelligence boys work outta, yeah? Looks like they turned him, sure enough."

"Do you have any concrete proof he turned?" Kelly asked.

"No."

"So why kill him? And, whose order was it to kill him? I don't recall hearing about any messages coming in."

"I know. I think Klepp either made the decision himself or was ordered to by his boss," O'Toole said.

"Jesus. If that's true, then you know what that means, right?"

O'Toole picked up his glass and drank some of the whisky Kelly poured again. He nodded as he put the glass down.

"He could receive orders to take us out as well and we wouldn't know it." Kelly paused a moment, then continued. "Christ. He could already have those orders."

"Shite, you're right. So what do we do? Kill him first?"

Kelly shook his head. "Too dangerous. Don't know what the German's reaction would be. I think I'd better get in touch with the council for instructions."

The two men sat quietly, thinking.

"So whadda we do now?" O'Toole asked, breaking the silence. "I mean, if Cafferty did break and turn, he could've told them anything. It could hurt us, especially me."

"I know. We got us another problem: if he did turn, then can't we trust anything he's given us since he was let go? And where does that put us with Klepp?" Kelly pointed out.

"Shite. This is a fuckin' mess, sure."

"I think we should lay low for a bit 'til we git some sorta idea what the bastards know."

O'Toole nodded his agreement.

"In the meantime, you git in touch with Cavanaugh. See if he's heard anything. Also, see if he can git us the name of the officer in charge and if they're on to you."

Michael Cavanaugh was another Irishman but not directly connected to the IRA. He had been living here for over twenty years. When the war broke out, he was employed as a stationary engineer in the building the navy commandeered as their headquarters on Barrington Street across from the Nova Scotian Hotel and train station. Like almost all Irishmen, he hated the British, so he was happy to provide information that he learned once he was approached by O'Toole.

"Okay, but we gotta be careful not to expose him. He's in a good position to do The Cause a lotta good here," O'Toole said.

"Gotta chance it. If Cafferty flipped, then we gotta know."

"I know, just pointin' it out."

Suddenly, sounds of yelling and crashing furniture filtered in from behind the closed door.

Kelly jumped up, almost knocking his chair over.

"Damn, not again," he said angrily. "There ain't a night goes by there ain't at least a coupla punch-ups."

"Need a hand?"

"Naw, thanks. I got a coupla men to handle it. We jus' gotta git it under control before the bulls show up. Don't need them stomping around."

He went to the door and reached over to a peg where an eight-inch long black leather sap hung. He pulled it down as he opened the door. The sounds of cursing and men fighting carried into the room.

"Outta the way ya sonofabitch," Kelly yelled as he raised the sap over his head.

Sean got up and went to the door in time to see a couple of big burly men manhandling a few sailors to the main entranceway with Kelly not too far behind them, a string of curses coming out of his mouth.

CHAPTER TWO

The grey dawn crept slowly over the distant horizon. The sky was heavy with low lying clouds threatening snow for the third day in a row. The seas looked black in the dim light and rolled with long swells broken by infrequent whitecaps from the stiffening icy wind coming out of the northeast. A few miles off the starboard side, the high face of Chebucto Head rose up, grim looking and cold, the surf crashing at its feet.

The entrance to Halifax Harbour appeared faintly visible in the waning darkness of the false dawn, the dark headland of Point Pleasant Park on one side, McNab's Island and the old Sherbrooke Tower lighthouse on Mauger's Beach on the other with tiny George's Island in the center and the ever present harbour defence boats tending the anti-submarine nets closing the harbour's entrance; the city beyond was under blackout conditions.

The small Cape Island boat, engine idling, rode up and down as the swells rolled slowly past. Mike Purcell, the owner and skipper of the boat stood beside his brother Ken. The two men were dressed in heavy black slickers and sou'wester hats and stood at the rail on the starboard side

hauling in the stiff hemp line, seawater flying off in a fine spray as it passed through the old wooden block hanging above them. After several moments, the lobster pot on the end of the line came into view.

A third man, Charlie Boudreau, a cigarette dangling from his lips, came and stood next to them and leaned over the rail. He grabbed the bent wood frame of the next pot with both hands and heaved it up and onto the rail, then guided it onto the deck. He quickly opened the small flap and reached inside, pulling out the three lobsters and tossing them into the holding bin fixed on the deck. Once empty of its catch, he dragged it to the stern and lifted it up onto the stack of a dozen similar pots piled on the open back three-quarters of the boat.

They worked in silence and harmony learned from years together; just another day on the water.

Meanwhile, the boat was already moving to the next buoy marker in the string.

"Here. What's that out there?" Ken Purcell said, raising an arm and pointing toward the mouth of the harbour.

"What? Where?" his brother said, looking.

"There."

"Yeah, yeah, I see it," he said. He saw something bobbing in the water about thirty feet away.

"Let's go take a gander. Might be sumthin' off one a them convoy ships. Might be worth sumthin'," Ken said.

Mike went to the wheel under the dodger and slipped the boat's motor into gear, spinning the wheel hard over to the port then quickly returned to midship. "Grab the hook an' git ready," he called over his shoulder.

Ken retrieved the long boat hook from under the gunwale.

"Hey, Charlie, give us a han' here will ya," Ken said, picking up the long pole with a large steel hook lashed to one end.

Mike manoeuvered the boat the thirty or so feet to the object, steering so the boat came up to it on his lee side. Meanwhile, the two men stood at the rail watching the thing bobbing in the waves, boat hook at the ready.

"Easy, Mike," Ken called out as he reached the pole out over the rail, dropping the hook onto the object and pulling it alongside. It was about six or seven feet long and wrapped in some sort of heavy burlap.

The two men leaned over the side and took hold of the thing and started to heave it up unto the rail then into the boat. It landed at their feet with a wet thud.

Mike pointed the boat back into the rising swell and then eased back on the throttle. He looked over at their mystery bundle lying on deck.

"Whadda we got?" he asked.

Ken started to unroll the bundle. After a few moments, he yanked on the hem and the body of a man rolled out landing on its back along with a half-dozen or so rocks.

He was dressed in a suit, open-necked shirt, and no shoes. His face was ghostly white and wrinkled from being in the water for a while. His lifeless eyes stared up into nothing.

"Jesus, Mary, and Joseph," Charlie muttered aloud, stepping back blessing himself with the sign of the cross.

"What? What is it?" Mike called from behind Ken.

"A body," Ken said, bending onto one knee for a closer look.

"Whaddya mean a body? Lemme see," he said, stepping over to his brother.

"Holy shit," he said, looking down at the body.

"Who'd ya think he was?" Charlie asked, still looking at it.

"Dunno. Might be a survivor maybe. You know, from one of them torpedoed ships we been hearin' about on the radio," Mike said.

"I don't think so," Ken said, "there ain't been anything on the radio for a coupla days. Besides, the tide's running out."

"So?" Mike said.

"So, it looks like this fella came from outta the harbour. An' look at 'im. He don't look like he's been in the water all that long."

"Jesus, you're right."

"And then there's this," Ken added, rolling the lifeless head to the side revealing the hair on the back. It was matted with caked blood and something else. "Poor bastard was shot."

"Tabernac," Charlie muttered.

"Whadda we do now?" Ken asked.

"Head back to the village an' call the cops," Mike said, standing up and heading back to the wheel. "Cover "im up an' secure him to the side."

"Whadda 'bout' the rest of da pots?" Charlie asked. They had only raised a little less than half their string and he needed this payday.

"Whaddya think?" Mike said, looking at his brother.

"Well, ya know the cops'll keep us in most a the day, so I suppose we oughta pull the rest before headin' in, and besides, that fella ain't goin' nowhere."

"Okay. Let's get to work. We should finish up by two. Jus' make sure he's tied in good," Mike said, turning the wheel and heading the boat back to the last marker.

Four and a half hours later, Mike Purcell eased around the point leading into Herring Cove and then alongside his wharf. Ken quickly scampered up the wooded frame to the top while Charlie stood at the bow and tossed a line up to him followed by another line from the aft end, securing the boat. Mike turned off the engine and went to the side of the boat, putting a foot on the gunwale.

"I'm goin' up to the house and call the police," Mike said to Ken.

"Yeah, sure. We'll be up soon as we finish here."

Ten minutes later, they had everything secured. They stepped off the boat and went up to the small house next to the road. An old '32 Ford pickup was parked in the dirt space beside the house. They went inside just as Mike was hanging up the phone. He and Charlie shed their slickers and boots. Jeannette, Mike's wife, had a pot of coffee brewed and was pouring out two mugs. They sat down at the kitchen table. Charlie pulled out his tobacco pouch and cigarette papers. After rolling a cigarette, he offered the pouch to Ken, who declined with a shake of his head.

"So? What gives?" Ken asked.

"They want us to meet them at the Waegwoltic on the arm in about an hour. "

"Fine by me," Charlie said, sitting down. Looking at Jeannette, he said with a smile, "Any chance of some of your great brown bread?"

"Good. At least we don't hafta deal with them guys at the nets and that gives us time to sell the catch. You called the navy boys yet?"

Mike shook his head. "Not yet. Wanted to wait an' see what the cops said. I'll call 'em now," he said, picking up the phone.

The police station was located in the basement of city hall, facing toward Duke Street. It was small and cramped and rapidly becoming inadequate and overwhelmed by the increasing daily pressures generated by the war, mostly from the influx of people, ships, and materials.

Fortunately, policing was being shared by the military, who took responsibility for their own, leaving the civilian and merchant seaman populations to the local authority.

I was sitting at my desk staring at the report I had just finished writing up. Earlier that day we, my partner and I, had arrested three men and two women who were trying to procure goods from the docks to be resold on the black market. We had been investigating them for the last two weeks and finally managed to insert a patrolman into one of the stevedore gangs. We eventually found out who they were along with some of their contacts on the docks. They set up the raid for this morning and, luckily, it went off without a hitch.

Incidents like this were becoming all too common these days as the demand for every form and type of consumer goods and, worse, drugs, especially cocaine, was growing. Most of this was allocated to the military and the convoy ships that led to frequent shortages for the rest of the population. It surprised me at times that there hadn't been more violence associated with these crimes.

Standing at the window, I caught a glimpse of myself reflected in the glass. Not too bad, I thought, turning a few inches to either side, appraising what I saw looking back. Forty-four, still had most of my hair, which had a few grey traces starting to accent the otherwise black hair. Standing at six foot and carrying a comfortable 210 pounds, I was still in good health. Yep. Not too bad at all.

I had been a member of the police force for more than twenty years. After my discharge from the army at the end of the last war where I served with the First Infantry Division, I travelled to the United States with an army buddy I served with in Europe. We eventually joined the Boston police department where I stayed on for a couple of years before returning to Nova Scotia. I knew I could not go back to my home in Cape Breton, not after all I'd seen and done. So I went to Halifax and joined the police.

The job proved to be a natural fit for me. I enjoyed my time as a patrolman where I earned a reputation as a cop who treated people fairly but also as a tough cop. When the opportunity arose, I advanced into the detective squad.

I met Louise, my wife, fifteen years ago and married her a year later. She gave me three kids since then—two boys, fourteen and twelve, and a girl, eight, the love of my life. Suddenly, the sharp blare of a transport truck's horn jolted me back from my reverie. I looked out onto Duke Street.

Military vehicles of every sort crammed the busy roadway while the sidewalks bustled with soldiers, sailors, airmen, and civilians. I saw the smattering of drunken servicemen weaving through the crowds, heading for the waterfront, some making passes at the young women as they moved by trying to avoid them. It was the times, I thought, shaking my head. Too many people. Not enough to do. I tried to understand. The stresses of the convoy and the uncertainty of living through the U-boat attacks, the harsh winter weather on the North Atlantic only to return back here, and the dullness of the city that it had become known for.

Just at that moment, the phone on my desk rang.

Picking up, I said into the mouthpiece, "Robichaud."

"Got a call here," the voice said on the other end. "Sez he found a body floatin' just outside the harbour by Herring Cove."

"Yeah, okay. Why ya tellin' me? Give him the navy's number. Sounds like it might be someone who fell overboard," I said.

"Yeah, normally ya might be right but, thing is, he sez the guy's been shot. One in the back of the head."

"Shit," I said. "Okay, patch him through."

There was a brief silence, then a click.

"This is Detective John Robichaud. I understand you found a body?"

"That's right," a man's voice said.

"Okay. First thing. What's your name?" I asked, sitting down and picking up my pen and pulling a notebook closer.

"Purcell. Mike Purcell. Me an' my brother own a small fishin' boat outta Herring Cove."

"Mr. Purcell, right. Okay, tell me about what you got."

"Well, we was out hauling our traps and Ken, that's my brother, he spots somethin' in the water. Well, I manoeuvered the boat over and then hauled it on board. That's when we saw it was a body. First, we figured it musta been some unlucky bastard from one a them foreign convoy ships, ya know? But then Ken, he points out that the tide was ebbing, so we figured it hadda come from inside the harbour, ya know?"

"I see. Was there anythin' on the body, like an ID or somethin' like that?" I asked.

"Nope, nothin'. We looked. That's when we saw the bullet hole in his head."

"Okay. And where is it now? The body?"

"Still lashed in the boat."

"I don't suppose there's any chance of you bringin' it into the city?"

"Be sorta hard, what with the gas rationin'." Purcell said.

"How about bringin' it to the Waegwoltic? Can you meet us there?"

"Yeah, that'd work okay, I s'ppose, since we'll be comin' in to sell the catch to the navy at the nets," Purcell said.

"Great. When do think you'll be there?"

There was a brief pause, then, "Say 'round' 'bout five."

I looked at my watch: three forty.

"Right. I'll meet you there. I'll be bringin' an ambulance along."

"Yeah, okay."

"See ya then," I said, then hung up.

The Waegwoltic was a sailing club located on the city side of the Northwest Arm about a quarter mile in from the mouth of the harbour. It was used by weekend boaters in peacetime, but now it had been taken over by the military and was occupied by the Nelson Sea Cadets who ran boat patrols in the Arm.

"What's that all about, Robie?" asked his partner, as he came over to his desk.

"A fisherman. Seems he caught somethin' more than fish this mornin'."

"Yeah?"

"Uh-huh, a body. Looks like might be a murder," I said. "We're meeting him at the Wag around five."

"I'll get a car ready," Duncan said.

"Okay. I'll call the hospital to have an ambulance ready to take the body in for an autopsy. We'll connect with them at the hospital and head out together. I'll meet you in the parkin' area after I head upstairs and let the boss know."

"Right," Duncan said.

Before heading upstairs, I picked up the phone again, I flipped through the small notebook that held all the numbers for the military offices. Once I found the number, I dialled. It took five minutes to get the clearance for Purcell to land his boat at the club and to get ready for our arrival.

When I was finished making my preparations, I grabbed my jacket and fedora and headed for the door. Five minutes later I was standing in front of Lieutenant Morrion's desk. Morrison was the duty commander.

"What's up?" he asked, looking up from a pile of papers.

"Just took a call from a fisherman out of Herring Cove. Sez he found a dead body in the water just outside the harbour past the submarine nets this mornin'. Looks like a suspicious death," I reported.

"Whaddya mean, suspicious? Suspicious? How?"

"Apparently, the man was shot in the back of the head."

"Yep, that'd do it all right," Morrison said. "I take you're off to look into it?"

I nodded. "Uh-huh. Me and Duncan. He's bringin' the body into the Wag. Pete and I are headin' down with an ambulance to take the body in for an autopsy. He'll be there around five."

"Okay. Keep me posted."

Meeting over, I turned and left, heading for the main entrance and out into the Grand Parade where the cars were parked.

The building that housed city hall was once the original site of Dalhousie University and the front area was the quad. It was now used by city and other vehicles for parking when here on official business.

Pete Duncan was already there waiting behind the wheel of the black unmarked police car, smoking a cigarette. I opened the passenger door and slipped onto the seat.

"Let's go," I said.

Duncan turned the ignition key and pressed the starter button on the floor. The big car's engine rumbled to life and he slipped the gear stick on the steering column into first, let out the clutch, and headed for the exit to Barrington Street.

Peter Duncan had been my partner for over two years. He was a steady, honest, and reliable cop. In his mid-thirties and still single, he cut a handsome figure that had an effect on many of the women he met. Only five feet four and weighing in at around 170 or so, he projected an impression of being an easy target. Big mistake. There are a good number of men in this city and outside who learned that lesson the hard way. Duncan was the middleweight champ of the force and was utterly fearless.

"Which way ya wanna go?" he asked, looking both ways. The street was thick with traffic. Mostly lorries and other vehicles and several trams. The sidewalk was equally blocked by pedestrians.

"We hafta stop at the hospital to hook up with the ambulance so quickest way'd be to just head down Barrington and up South."

"Okay," Pete said, flipping on the siren as he eased the car out into the mess of traffic.

We made our way quickly through the traffic as it yielded to the siren. Fifteen minutes later we reached the Victoria General Hospital, or as it was commonly called, the VG. He turned off the siren as he turned into the ambulance area.

The white ambulance was parked, waiting. Inside there were two medics dressed in their white uniforms. One got out when he recognized us and came over. I rolled my window down as he stepped up and leaned in.

"What's up?" he asked.

"We got a dead body. A fisherman found it floatin' in the harbour this mornin'. He's bringing in to the Waegwoltic. I need you guys to deliver it to the morgue for an autopsy," I said.

"Okay. So, how come you guys are handlin' this? Ain't somethin' like that usually handled by the military?"

"Looks like this one's murder."

"No shit." The attendant whistled.

"No shit. Let's go. It'll be dark soon and I want to get back as soon as possible."

"Okay."

Pete headed the car back out to South Street and turned right, the ambulance moving in behind us. He put the siren on again and traffic parted as we drove down the middle of the street as he led the way to Jubilee Road.

We arrived at the club just over ten minutes later. We were met by four young sea cadets who flagged us down. Pete slowed to a stop, turning off the siren and rolling his window down.

Mike and his crew had finished off-loading their catch to the motor launch they were tied up to and were waiting for the young navy lieutenant to pass them their payment.

"Thanks," Mike said, taking the wad of bills the officer passed across to him.

"See you next time," the young man said as his crew let go the lines holding them together.

Mike went to the wheel and shifted the motor out of idle and turned the boat's head toward the Northwest Arm. Ten minutes later, he was easing his boat alongside the platform where a couple of sea cadets waited to take his lines. Once secured alongside, he shut the motor off. No point wasting petrol, he thought. Mike saw the uniformed officer walking down the ramp from the boathouse. He reached under the top of the console and pulled out his papers, then stepped onto the platform.

"Capt'n," he said, passing the papers to him.

The officer took the papers and scanned them.

"Mr. Purcell. My name is Chapman," he said. "I understand you had quite a day of fishin'."

"Could say that, yeah. So, I guess ya know what this is about, then?"

Chapman nodded. "Yes. The police have contacted me."

Just at that moment, Ken saw the black Pontiac sedan round the corner at the top of the hill. followed by an ambulance. "Looks like they're here," he called from the deck of the boat.

Charlie was down on a knee untying the body.

A moment later they saw two men dressed in civilian clothes round the corner of the boathouse and approach them.

"Police. We're expected," a man said to a fresh faced boy, who looked to be about sixteen years old dressed in the black navy uniform and brimless, flat black pusser hat. He sported the rank of petty officer, three white stripes topped by two crossed anchors on a sleeve.

"Yes, sir," the boy said. "Just head over that way. Captain Chapman is down at the dock on the other side of the boathouse. The boat you're expecting just pulled alongside a couple of minutes ago."

"Thanks," Pete said, easing the car forward and waving the ambulance to follow. The vehicles rolled over the gravel road leading to the boathouse.

We stopped, got out, and walked to the dock. The fishing boat was tied to the small pier normally used to launch skulls and paddle boats. Several cadets stood around watching while a man in uniform with four gold bars on the bottom the sleeves stood looking at papers and talking to another man. Two other men stood at the rail of the boat. All three wore black slickers.

"Captain Chapman?" I said when I stepped on the platform.

"Yes. You must be the detective that called," he said, stepping forward with a hand extended. A man followed behind him wearing an oilskin slicker and boots. Looked like the fisherman that called.

"Yes, sir. This is Detective Duncan," I answered, accepting the hand.

"Mr. Purcell?" I said, looking at the fisherman.

"Yeah, you Robichaud?" Mike answered, accepting the other's offered hand.

"That's right. Where's the body?"

"Over there," he said, pointing back at his boat. "That's my crew."

"Let's walk over and you can start filling me in on what we got." I turned and told the ambulance attendant standing at the corner of the building to bring the gurney down to the boat.

Mike Purcell led the two detectives over to the boat. Ken and Charlie had untied the ropes holding the body against the side and it now lay on its back with the tarp loosely on top.

I stepped onto the deck and bent down on a knee, pulling back the tarp and rolling the head toward me.

Duncan stepped on board behind me and was leaning over my shoulder.

"Jesus, Robie, is that who I think it is?" he said.

"Yep, Denny Cafferty. Looks like the boys over in intelligence aren't gonna be too happy about this."

"Whaddya mean?" Duncan asked.

"Right, forgot, you didn't know. Cafferty was working with them as an informant."

"No shit. How'd you find that out?"

"Lieutenant Morrison told me a couple of days ago. Thought I should know. He figured we'd cross his path someday because of his connections. Anyway, I meant to tell you but forgot because we were settin' up the raid on the gang we just arrested and we hadn't heard anything 'bout Cafferty for over a week."

"Okay, so, you think his pals found out and did this?"

"An IRA hit? Hmm, yeah, maybe," I said.

I took another quick look at the body, then stood up, signalling the medics to come down and collect the body as I stepped back on the dock with Duncan following me.

"Get the body to the morgue as soon as you can. Tell them that I need an autopsy done as quick as they can. Oh, and tell them that the bullet might still be inside the skull and to get it out and send it with their report."

"Okay," one of the medics said, stepping down onto the deck.

"Thanks again for your cooperation. If we need to talk again I'll call."

"No problem," Purcell said, shaking his hand.

On the way back to our car, Pete asked, "You gonna call the navy?"

"Nope. That's Morrison's job."

CHAPTER THREE

Lieutenant Michael Parks sat in a chair next to a closed glass panelled door with the words *Cmdr. J. M. Willis, Director Operations*, stencilled in black on it. He was responsible for all matters of security in the port, especially as they related to convoys.

He was dressed in the traditional black uniform of the navy: neatly pressed cuffed pants, double-breasted jacket with polished brass buttons, white shirt, black tie. A single light blue band circled the bottom of each sleeve.

He joined the Royal Navy three years ago right out of Oxford in 1935. He was initially trained as a signals officer and after a short tour on a destroyer, was reassigned to naval intelligence Communications. A year later he was sent to Halifax where he'd been for the last eight months.

At twenty-four, he was one of many young men recently assigned to this department, most of whom had been posted in a number of theatres of operation—a necessity of the time. He had an athletic build for his height, good looks, and was five-nine. He also projected an air of confidence without the usual aloofness so many of his brother officers had.

He sat with a leg crossed over a knee, watching the attractive young woman sitting behind the desk set to one side of the door as she busied ıerself with a pile of papers. He knew she was aware of his appreciative stares.

Her name was Susan Oakley, a civilian clerk assigned to Commander Willis. She looked like she was about twenty or twenty-two. A beautiful, clear complexion was framed wonderfully by her shoulder-length ash-blonde hair and she had applied just enough red lipstick to finish it all off. She wore a short-sleeved beige-coloured blouse buttoned at the neck with a red ribbon tied under the tatted collar. Many of the lads had tried and failed to snap her up. He had yet to roll the dice.

The office was a beehive of activity. It was a cramped space with desks being made to fit as best as possible. Overhead, two rows of lights glared harsh and white, giving the room a cold feel. A bank of grey filing cabinets sat padlocked and bolted against one wall with steel rods set into the handles. A map of the North Atlantic covered a third of an adjacent wall, showing both the eastern half of North America and the western part of Europe. Uniformed men and women were busy going over papers or talking on the phone.

Just then, the phone on her desk rang. She picked it up after the first ring.

"Yes, sir. He's here waiting," she said after a moment passed, her voice clear with just a musical hint to it. "Yes, sir."

She hung up and looked at him. "He's ready to see you now, Lieutenant."

He stood up and said thank you, then, after a quick rap on the glass, turned the knob and entered the office, closing the door behind him.

"Sir," he said, coming to attention at the front of the desk.

"Parks," the older man sitting there said, "Sit. Cigarette?"

"No thanks, sir. Never quite got the habit," Parks said as he sat down.

"Good for you. Filthy things really, but somehow help one to relax. Cafferty. Isn't he one of yours?"

"Yes, sir. We picked him up about three months ago. IRA. We suspected him of passing information along to either one of his IRA contacts here, or possibly a German agent. We managed to turn him."

"Hmm, well, he turned up dead this morning. Some fishermen found him floating just outside the nets. Seems he was shot in the head."

"I see," Parks said. "How do we know for certain it's him?"

"Our contact on the police force, seems he got wind of it when they got the call. A couple of detectives took the call and identified the body. What do we know about his connections or contacts here?" Willis asked.

"Not a lot unfortunately. We know that he was spending time with several local Irishmen as well as some known criminals but our investigations didn't turn up anything significant for us to act on. We think he was moving in those circles to gain access to information on cargoes and ships on the waterfront. We think he was passing information to one of these two men but can't prove it yet. We've got them under surveillance for now."

"Interesting. What about this German agent? Is there one here?"

"It is looking like it's a definite possibility. However, we aren't completely in the dark. We recently received information from our sources in the FBI in New York. Apparently, they learned that a German national recently arrived from Berlin at their embassy five months ago. They think he's with the Abwehr. They lost track of him a couple of months ago and think he has left New York. He may have entered Canada through Montreal and may have made his way here. We have a solid description of him but no name. We've been hoping that this agent makes contact with the Irishmen. It's the main reason we haven't hauled them in yet."

"Hmm, I see. I guess it was to be expected that the Abwehr would try and place someone here sooner or later, although I am a bit surprised it took the Americans so long to learn of his connections to German Intelligence. What steps are you taking to find him?"

"Based on our efforts, we have concluded that he would only have two options for relaying any information he gets: by phone or wireless to an offshore vessel, most likely a U-boat. We've contacted the phone company and have people placed inside their communications center monitoring all long-distance calls. As to the wireless possibility, we have set up listening posts at Hartland Point, McNab's, and York Redoubt. If he transmits within ten miles of the port we should be able to triangulate his position."

"Very good," Willis said. "Why only ten miles?"

"The prevailing view is that travel any farther away would be too problematic. About Cafferty, sir."

"Yes. His body was collected by the local police and taken to the VG for an autopsy."

"Do you want us to take over this investigation?" Parks asked.

"No, I don't think we need to allocate resources to this, do you?"

"Probably not, sir, but he was an asset we were using."

"And you think that they may stumble onto something relevant to your group?"

"It's a possibility, yes, sir," Parks said.

"Right, I think the solution is to put you in contact with their lead investigator as, say, a liaison. Set it up as soon as you leave here." He flipped open a file on his desk and looked down at it.

"The head detective's name is John Robichaud. A good cop and detective by all accounts. A veteran of the last one. You two should work well together."

"Yes, sir. How much should I share with him? He will want to know why we are interested and why we want to be involved in what to him, may just be a simple case of murder?"

"I trust to your judgement. Good luck. Report every couple of days on the investigation."

"Yes, sir," Parks said, standing up. He turned and left the office.

Pete Duncan and I arrived back at the station just before six. Traffic was stiff on the trip back from the Waegwoltic Club, even with the siren on. We got caught behind a ten-vehicle transport heading for the navy dockyard.

"Whaddya think?" Pete Duncan asked as he manoeuvered the car through the traffic.

"I'm thinking we don't need the headache right now."

"Amen to that. But ya know we'll be stuck with it, right? And, what about the navy guys? Think they'll butt in?"

"Probably. Hell, if we're lucky, they'll take over and we'll be off the hook."

"We can't be that lucky," Pete said, smiling.

"Yeah."

"So, if ya figure we're stuck with it, whaddya figure?" Pete asked again.

"First, we pull everything we got on Cafferty. See if we can make any connections," I said. "We know that he was busy with some of the local villains. Maybe we can tie him to someone. Oh, and see if we can tie him to Kelly."

"You think this might've been an IRA job? The shot in the back of the head sounds like what they do."

"Hmm, maybe. The Mafia uses the same method. I remember a couple of similar cases back when I was in Boston. But, I don't think it was mob related."

"Yeah?"

I nodded. "Yeah. They aren't here."

"Okay, but what about some of the local gangs? Think Cafferty might've crossed one of them?"

"Again, maybe. We know he was runnin' a few deals that might've stepped on some toes. But none of the gangs have shown this level of violence before, so I don't know."

"Always a first time, I guess," Pete said as he pulled across traffic into the parking area at city hall.

Once back in the squad room, I went to my desk and called home to let my wife know I'd be late getting home. Pete went to a filing cabinet and opened a drawer.

While talking with my wife, I saw the note on his desk. I picked it up and read it. *Call Lt. Michael Parks at Naval HQ.* A phone number was written under the name. That was quick, I thought, saying good-bye to my wife after telling her I loved her.

I depressed the disconnect button on the phone and held it down for a few seconds, then released it and dialed the number.

"Lieutenant Parks," a young sounding voice said into his ear.

"Robichaud. You called?"

"Ah, yes. Thanks for getting back so quick. I understand that you have a body that was discovered outside the harbour this morning?"

"Uh-huh. Denny Cafferty. One of yours, I understand."

"Uh, yes, but we shouldn't discuss that over an open line. Is it possible to meet up with you, say, in a half an hour? There are some things we need to discuss."

"Okay. Where?" I said.

"Your office?"

"Yeah, okay. You been here before?"

"Yes. You're in the basement, right?"

"Right, I'll let the desk officer know you're coming. See you in half an hour."

"Half an hour," Parks said, then hung up.

"Hey, Pete. We got company coming," I called out, picking up the phone again. When I connected to the front desk, I let the duty officer know about Parks's arrival and to send him back.

"Let me guess, navy?"

"In half an hour." I nodded. "A Lieutenant Michael Parks. Any luck over there?"

"Not a lot," Duncan said, pulling a file and coming over to his desk and sitting down. "He might not have been busy, but he sure knew who to hook up with, take a look." He passed the file across the desk.

I took the file and scanned the top page.

"You're right. He seems to have gone right to the worst of the bunch, I'll give him that," he said.

"Did you note one of his known contacts?"

"Uh-huh, Kelly," I said.

"Still think none of those people listed in there would hesitate to put one in someone's head?"

I looked at him and said, "Maybe."

After several moments, I closed the file and sat back.

"Question is, what was a suspected IRA soldier doin' with them? I mean, sure they're all villains, but I wouldn't've thought they had any IRA sympathies."

"Patriotic thugs. Who'd've thought!" Pete said, a hint of sarcasm in his voice.

"One thing I've learned about criminals over the years on the job, Pete, is that they aren't much different from us. They have families they support and love and have to pay their bills like the rest of us."

"Yeah, I suppose that's true. Never really think of them that way. Too busy wanting to put them away."

"Yeah, me too. I think I'll pop upstairs and have a chat with the boss. See if he's got anythin' else from the navy on Cafferty he can share before Parks shows up. You dig up what we got on those other names on the list, especially Kelly. Maybe we can find something that explains why Cafferty was working with them."

"Okay," Pete said, getting up at the same time as me.

"Come," Morrison called from behind the closed door. I sometimes thought he lived in there because he spends over twelve to fourteen hours a day working.

"Whaddya got?" he asked when I sat down in front of the desk.

"It's definitely Denny Cafferty. He was shot in the back of the head. Looks like it was done within the last twenty-four hours. No more than thirty-six, I figure. Looks like a mob style hit you see in the States. Could also be one of his Irish pals. You know, the IRA."

"You think they got something going on here?"

"Possible, yeah, especially if the reports are true that they've gotten into bed with the Nazis."

"Hmm, where is he now?"

"The VG. I ordered an autopsy and also asked them to look for the bullet."

Morrison gave me a slightly puzzled look.

"No exit wound."

"Ah, go on," he said.

"We checked our file on him and nothing, except that he appears to be associated with some of our more notorious criminals. Pete's checking what we got on them to see if we can find out what the connection might be. He was also connected to Iain Kelly."

"Kelly, huh. No real surprise there."

"Yeah. What we're thinking too. Also, a Lieutenant Parks called. Wants to meet us. He's on the way over."

"Yeah, I know Parks. Don't let his young looks fool you. He's a good man. I got a feelin' that his people will want him in on this case. You okay with that?"

"Not a problem for me. If that's the case, you have anythin' you can fill me in on, besides what I already know?"

"Hmm. Let's wait on that, okay? You talk to Parks first and I'll make a call. When you and Parks are done, come up. If I get the go-ahead, we'll talk."

"Okay, thanks," I said, standing up.

"One more thing."

"Sir?"

"Play nice with him. We're on the same side."

"I always play nice...sir," I said with a sly smile.

Lieutenant Parks was sitting in front of my desk when I returned to the squad room. Pete was just passing him a mug of coffee.

Morrison was right: he did look awfully young for someone doing his line of work. I stood at my desk and reached across, offering him my hand. He had a surprisingly firm grip.

"You must be Parks," I said, sitting down and signalling Pete to pull up a chair.

"Yes, sir," he answered. "And you must be Detective Robichaud."

"Right, and call me Robie. This is my partner, Detective Pete Duncan."

"Greetings, and it's just Pete," Duncan said, shaking the young man's hand.

"So, what can the police do for naval intelligence?" I asked.

"Thanks. I'm Michael. I think this may be a case of what we can do for each other."

"Denny Cafferty," I said.

"Yes. We caught him a while back as part of another operation that I can't discuss. We were alerted to him from our brothers at MI5 and Special Branch in England by way of diplomatic channels in New York. Seems he was involved in a bombing campaign run by the IRA that targeted major cities there. Anyway, his last mission failed and he just managed to escape capture. Special Branch learned that he had been secreted out of Ireland and sent to Canada. That's where they lost contact with him. It wasn't until we caught him here that we realized who he was and that was when we turned him."

"A major coup for you guys, considering that these IRA guys, especially if they're hard-core, are pretty anti-British," I said.

"True, but when we explained his options to him he opted to play with us."

I had a good idea what the options were. I had read reports on how the British dealt with the IRA when they caught one of them, especially bombers. Not very pleasant.

"So, are you here to share information with us?" I asked, going right to the heart of the matter.

Parks sat back, crossed his legs, and studied the detective. He already knew quite a bit about the man from records back at headquarters. The department had opened files on civilians who were directly involved with anything to do with the war, especially the police.

"Perhaps, it would be easier if you told me what you already have. Then I'll be in a better position to know what I can share," Parks said.

"Yeah, okay. I get it. First, what we *know* isn't much. In fact, what you just told us is more than we actually have on Cafferty. He kept his head down and didn't draw a lot of attention from us. He only came to our attention through his criminal activities and, of course, that memo you guys sent to us."

"What about these contacts? Who were they?"

"Mostly bad guys: bootleggers, black marketeers, smugglers, thugs. Oh yeah, there was this one guy, an Irishman. Sean O'Toole," Pete put in.

"Oh yes, him. We know about him. No Germans?" Parks asked.

"Not that we know about. You saying we got a German spy operating here in the city?" I asked.

"We have received information from the FBI in New York that a German arrived a while back at their embassy there but they lost him shortly after. They think he entered Canada through Montreal. We think he may have made his way here."

"That's it? That's all you guys got?" Pete asked.

"Unfortunately, yes," Parks said. "We were woefully unprepared at the outbreak of the war. We have been scrambling to catch up ever since."

"Jesus. How fucking hard is it to find one German! He would kinda stand out," Pete said.

"Not necessarily. We know that Hitler ordered his intelligence organization to recruit agents who spoke fluent English to be implanted in the US and here, in Canada. And before you ask, we know about this because a few have been captured and talked."

"Back to Cafferty," I said, cutting Pete off before he could say any more. "You mean he knew who this agent was and was passing information to him?"

Parks nodded.

"Let me guess. When you picked Cafferty up you guys thought you had a chance to use him to pass false information, hoping to misdirect any U-boats."

Parks nodded again, looking impressed. "That was the plan."

"So what happened?"

"Somehow, they found out and killed him," Parks said. "At least that would be our guess."

"Okay," I said. "That kinda fits with what we're thinking. The shot in the back of the head is kind of a signature method of killing used by some organizations."

"Quite right. We know that it's a standard method of execution used by the IRA."

"And the Mafia. Saw it before when I worked in Boston. So, what do you want us to do? I assume that's part of the reason you're here, right? To get our help."

Parks smiled. He liked this man and could work easily with him.

"Yes."

"So, you're not here to take the case away from us then?" Pete asked.

"No. We don't have the resources or expertise to undertake a murder investigation. Our only interest is in locating this German agent. Besides, you know the local area better than we do, from a non-military point of view, that is," Parks said.

"So, this isn't just a murder investigation? You want us to help you find this German?" Pete asked.

"Yes, exactly. I'm hoping that we can work together in achieving our respective goals," Parks said.

"Makes sense," I put in. "Just how do you see this partnership working exactly?"

"Simple enough, really. You do what you would normally do in such a case. I will stand aside until such time as you learn anything about this agent. Then my department will concern itself with him. Also, I will provide whatever you need from our side as the situation warrants."

"What if this agent is the killer?" Pete asked.

"He would still become the sole responsibility of the security service."

"Bugger that," Pete said. "What you're saying is that if we find this guy and he's the killer, we turn him over to your people who will try and use him in exchange for some sorta deal, maybe even immunity."

"Simply put, but yes, you got the picture. I know it seems a bad deal to you, but it is war after all, and we are up against it so far and need any and every edge we can get. You will have to be content knowing that you solved your case and let it go. Assuming this agent proves to be the killer, that is."

"That's clear enough," I said. "It's obvious we don't have a choice in this, so let's get on with it. What can you tell us about this agent? We need to have something so we know what we're looking for and get an idea who he may be working with locally."

"Fair enough. So far, we don't have much, other than knowing that he's here and has been for a while. We know he came via Montreal from New York, as I have already said. We were able to learn from Cafferty that he has been sending radio messages offshore, probably to a U-boat. We are taking steps to deal with that aspect. We also learned that the information he's sending has been coming from local sources."

"Like Cafferty's contacts," I said.

Parks nodded. "Yes. We now know that he had connected with certain people here with access to information, mostly related to the convoys: number of ships, cargoes, and related information."

"Any names?" Pate asked.

"We have several, but have learned that they weren't the ringleaders."

He opened his valise and extracted a file and opened it. He pulled out a sheet of paper and passed it across to me.

"These are the names that Cafferty provided. I'm sure you will recognise some, if not all, of them."

I took the sheet and quickly scanned the short list of typed names, then passed it to Duncan.

"We know a couple of these guys. We got a similar list. Can we hang on to this?"

Parks nodded. "Certainly. It's a copy."

"Mosta these guys are just street toughs," Pete said, putting the sheet of paper on the desk. "Usually work the docks when not muggin' some poor bastard. Some do odd jobs for a few of the bosses, like collectin' on loans, gamblin' debts."

"That was our assessment as well. Cafferty said he never met with these 'bosses' directly."

"You have anything that suggests that these guys are working with the German?"

"No. We think it's entirely possible that no one on that list knew about the information Cafferty was gathering or that he was passing it along to him."

"Hmm, you're probably right about that. These guys might be villains but I doubt they'd do anything treasonous, at least not the ones I've dealt with," I said. "But then again...who knows. They *are* criminals."

"Quite so," Parks added.

"Okay. You got anything else to share?"

"At this moment, no. We will provide you with anything you need... within the limits of security, that is."

"I understand. Okay," I said, standing up. "If you have a few more minutes to spare, my boss wants you stop by his office before you leave."

"Certainly," Parks said, standing up. "Oh, yes, one more thing. It would be best if we could keep this business under wraps. No press."

"That might be tricky. We don't have that many murders here, so the press is gonna be all over this," I said.

"I understand, but do try. It wouldn't do having the general public..." Parks said, leaving the obvious inference hanging.

"We'll do our best, but no promises. If that's it, I'll take you up. Pete, take that list and dig out everythin' we have on the ones we know. Also, call our friend down at the union, see if he's got anythin' on the ones we got nothin' on. I'll be back in a few minutes."

"Okay," Pete said.

"Nice to have met you," Parks said, extending his hand to Duncan.

"Yeah, you too," Pete said, taking the offered hand.

I returned to the squad room ten minutes later.

"Any luck?" I asked, looking at Duncan who was flipping through a filing cabinet.

"No. Nothin' yet. Don't mean there's nothin' there," Duncan answered without looking away.

"Okay. Forget it for now. It's gettin' late so let's call it a day."

"Works for me. I been thinkin' maybe we should bring O'Toole in. Shake him down a little. See what comes loose."

"Hmm, yeah, maybe. Let me think on it. Whaddya got on for tonight? Another conquest?"

Duncan chuckled as he closed the cabinet drawer. He stepped over to his desk and picked up his coat and hat.

"Naw. Had a bit of a dry spell lately. Thought I'd stop in at the Bon Ton. See what's shakin'."

The Bon Ton was an all-night dine and dance club located on Barrington Street down near Sackville. It was a popular spot for a lot of the naval ratings looking for a bit of fun and a pretty girl to chat up.

"Okay. Good luck. Just make sure you're here at seven thirty."

"Yes, Dad," Duncan said, flipping a salute as he left the squad room.

CHAPTER FOUR

The next day dawned under a heavily overcast grey sky. A long dark fog bank was visible on the near horizon. A good day for ships coming and going from the harbour. A bad one for the U-boats, unless they got real lucky, which they all too often did. The air was damp and raw, the kind that penetrates into your bones. Another typical March day.

I arrived at the station at five minutes to eight. The area in front of the duty officer was full of people, mostly patrolmen coming and going as the shifts changed. There was also what was becoming the usual press of servicemen and foreigners arrested during the night and being released in the morning. Unfortunately for some, the cells would be their best chance of shelter for the night.

I made my way through the mob to a door past the duty officer's desk, who nodded at me as I went by.

"Hey, Detective," someone yelled.

I stopped and looked around, spotting the man who called out over near the entrance. He was struggling to push his way through the crowd. I recognized him immediately: Gerry Cunningham, a reporter for the *Chronicle.*

"Hang on a minute. I got a coupla questions for ya 'bout a body in the harbour," he yelled.

I turned away and headed through the door leading to my office.

The squad room was busy with the shift change. I saw Pete Duncan already sitting at his desk poring over a small stack of files. I appreciated his dedication to the job.

"Cunningham's outside waitin' to pigeonhole us, so be careful what you say," I said, hanging up my hat and coat on one of the coat hooks affixed to the wall.

"Okay," Pete said, looking up. "He's quick on the spot. How do ya figure he found out so quick?"

"Yeah. He gets around right enough. My guess would be either one of the fishermen or maybe one of the ambulance people hopin' to make a buck sellin' a story. Don't much matter since it was bound to get out sooner or later. We jus' gotta try an' contain it by not givin' him anywhere to go. By the way, did ya get lucky?" I asked.

Pete Duncan sat back and looked over at me with a sly grin on his face.

"Right. Stupid question. Any joy there?" I said, indicating the files as I headed for the coffee urn.

"Not much. There's a coupla things Nothin' that would ring any bells though," Pete said, getting up and following me to my desk, taking a chair in front of it. "So? You give anymore thought 'bout bringin' O'Toole in?"

"Uh-huh. I guess it's the only thing we got at the moment so, yeah, let's find him and have a talk," I said, sitting down. "We know where he is?"

"I'll make a few calls and check with the desk sergeant. Maybe he's got somethin' from the patrol boys."

"Okay. I think I'll take a run up to the hospital, see what the autopsy turned up."

Just then the phone on my desk rang.

"Robichaud," I said when he picked up.

"Robie, it's me, Jake. One of the night shift beat cops reported somethin' might be of interest to you."

"Okay. Send him back," I said, then hung up.

A moment later, a young looking uniformed cop stepped into the squad room. I waved him over.

"Detectives," he said when he reached the desk.

"Mornin'," I said. "The desk sergeant said you have somethin' for us?"

"Yes, sir. I don't know if it's important or not, but I figured I better let somebody know," the cop said.

"That's okay, just tell us and we'll figure it out. By the way, what's your name?"

"Mike MacDonald, sir."

"Okay, Mike, talk."

"Well, sir, I got the graveyard shift and my beat is down around Ocean Terminals. Anyway, one of the neighborhood locals I know down there let me know that he thought he saw some men the other night."

"Whaddya mean, 'some men'? There's always men down around the docks at all hours these days," Pete said.

"Yes, sir. But he said he saw these three men headed into a corner at the end of one of the rail spurs down by shed twenty-six. According to him, they didn't look like dockworkers."

"Okay, so they didn't look like workmen?" Pete said.

"Yes, sir. Anyway, I decided to take a look in the place where he said they went. When I checked the area, I discover a lot of blood. It was mostly dried but it was definitely blood."

"And where exactly was this?" I asked.

"Down at the end of the spur at pier twenty-six. I reported this to the sergeant and he sent the day man down to secure the spot in case you want to take a look."

"Good work. What's the name of your contact and how can we reach him?"

"Marcel LeBlanc. Lives on Bishop Street, but you can get him over at Ocean Terminals. He works at General Fisheries. Night shift mostly."

"Well, that answers the question why he was in that area so late," Pete pointed out.

"Okay, thanks, Mike. You did good on this. I won't forget it," I said.

The young cop looked please and almost beamed.

"Thanks. If that's it, I think I'll check out and head home," MacDonald said, turning on his heel and walking off.

"Good cop," I said after MacDonald left.

Pete looked at me and said, "Guess we're headin' for the docks, then?"

"Uh-huh. Let's get the lab guys to meet us there. I finished off my coffee, then set the mug down.

"You call them and set it up while I go upstairs. Meet you at the car."

"Okay," Pete said.

Twenty minutes later, we found a parking spot halfway down a row of railcars sitting next to a shed. We spotted another marked police car parked nearer the road with its flasher blipping. We got out and walked to the end of the row of cars where we were greeted by a uniformed patrolman and two plainclothes cops we recognized from our crime lab—Detectives Ferguson and Morris. There were also several civilians dressed in work clothes standing nearby, one was arguing with the uniformed cop.

I stepped over to one of the lab guys.

"Hey, Mo, whadda we got?" Detective Morris was down on his knees scrapping something off the ground.

"Robie. Pete," he said without looking up. "Blood. Looks like a lot of it. We also found a shell casing over there under that railcar. I'm guessin' that's of interest to you, yeah?"

"Good guess," I said. "You got any idea what might've happened here yet?"

"Best I kin figure is somebody was shot."

"Gee, blood and a shell casing, hmm. Whaddya think the chances are?" Pete said, chuckling.

"Smart-ass," Morris said, standing up, looking briefly at Duncan then back to me. "We might have more to tell ya later when we finish searchin' the area."

"Okay. Let me know as soon as you get anything and, hey, thanks," I said.

"No sweat. Chance to get outta the office."

The sounds of the argument got louder coming from the small crowd being held back by the cop.

"Okay, okay. What's all the yellin' about?" I asked when I arrived at the scene, Pete close behind me.

"What da fuck's goin' on? We got work ta do an' you guys got the area shut down," said a large burly man dressed in a thick black overcoat and wearing a salt and pepper woolen hat pulled down over his right ear, common among working men, especially on the waterfront.

"And who are you?" I asked.

"Clark. I'm the dock foreman," the man said.

"Okay, Mr. Clark, my name is Robichaud. The area is closed and under investigation."

"Yeah? Investigation for what?"

I looked at the man. "I think you should take your guys and head over to the canteen. Get yourselves some coffee. We'll send someone over when it's clear to go to work."

"This is bullshit," Clark said. "I gotta timetable, you know. That ship there hasta be ready to leave by tonight."

"Can't be helped. Look, we should be done in an hour latest. Then you can be back to work, okay?"

"No, it ain't. I'm gonna hafta report this back to the hall."

"Thanks for your cooperation. Now move along," I said, ignoring the inference Clark was making and turning away.

"Hey, Detective. Whaddya got?" It was Cunningham again.

I turned partly around and said, "We got nothin' to say at this time."

"Word is that there's a lotta blood down there. That mean someone was killed?"

I stepped over to the line and stood inches away from Cunningham's face.

"I said, we got nothin' to say, got it? Now you can write whatever you might be guessin', but I can guarantee it'll die over at Bedford Row. You get me?"

Cunningham looked like he wanted to press me but decided to keep his mouth shut and backed off. He knew that we could make a call to the censor's office and shut his story down.

"Pete," I said, turning away from the line and heading back to the crime scene. "You stay here. Make sure those guys leave, Then if the lab guys don't have anything new, head over to General. See if this LeBlanc fella is workin' today. If not, then head to his home. You got the address. Get everythin' you can. I'm gonna head over to see Parks. I got the feeling he knows more about O'Toole than he's let on. You take the car. I'll catch a tram or walk back."

"Okay," Duncan said.

Naval headquarters was located in a nondescript redbrick building across from Cornwallis Park on Barrington Street. All the services had laid claim to specific properties to use as their headquarters. Originally, this building was home to the Navy League but was commandeered by the navy at the outbreak of the war. Made sense since the Hotel Nova Scotian, the rail station, and Ocean Terminals were also across from it. This was also the location where the navy ran all convoy planning.

It took me about fifteen minutes to walk from the suspected crime scene to the building. As I walked up past the park, I couldn't help noticing the number of sailors and merchant seamen and several young women that filled the park, even this early in the day. But then there were not a lot of places for them to go and relax from the stresses of the North Atlantic and the U-boats.

Halifax was not a welcoming or friendly city for these men. I knew that at some point, the city would pay the price for its shortsightedness; only question was...by how much!

There were quite a few people, mostly naval ratings and officers along with civilians, going in and out the main door. When I entered the building, I was stopped by a sailor wearing an armband with the letters *SP* on it in white. He wore a white web belt around his waist with a service revolver hanging on it. He also carried a British Sten gun, which he held across his chest.

"I'd like to see Lieutenant Parks," I said, showing the man my identification card.

"Go over there. See Lieutenant Kennedy. He's the duty officer," the sailor said, pointing at a small desk near the bottom of a staircase.

I stepped past the sailor and went over to the desk where a man sat dressed in a black double-breasted jacket with a double row of brass buttons down the front, four to a row. He was bent over an open ledger writing something.

"Excuse me," I said.

The officer looked up. "Yes. Can I help you?"

"Yes. I want to see Lieutenant Parks, please."

"And you are?"

"Detective John Robichaud, Halifax Police Department." I held out my identification out, which was still in my hand. The officer took the wallet and carefully read it before passing it back.

"One moment, Detective," he said, reaching for the phone on the desk. He dialled three numbers.

"Sorry to bother you, sir, but I have a police officer here wanting to see you," he said into the phone. Then, after a brief pause, he said, "Robichaud."

I stood for a few moments before the officer said "Yes, sir," then hung up.

"He will be down momentarily. He asks that you wait for him," he said, pointing to a row of wooden chairs against the wall under a couple of windows.

"Thanks," I said, heading for a chair.

Five minutes later, I spotted Lieutenant Parks coming down the stairs.

"Detective," Parks said when he reached him, his hand out.

"Lieutenant," I said, accepting the extended hand. It was a friendly handshake. "And it's Robie, remember."

"Sorry. So? What brings you to my world?"

"It looks like we've found where Cafferty may have been shot. But that's not why I'm here. I thought maybe you could let me have more information on Sean O'Toole as well as anything else you have on the IRA here."

"Hmm, yes, I see," Parks said. "I suppose you had better come through."

Parks turned and led me over to the desk and signed me in, then took me up the stairs.

"You say you might have found where Cafferty was killed?"

"Uh-huh. Someone reported something fishy to one of our beat cops who then went to investigate it. That's when he found a large bloodstain. Our crime scene guys are investigating the site now."

"I see. And what do you think?"

"I think it's where he was shot. We don't get a lot of shootings, so chances are that it's likely to do with Cafferty."

"Makes sense," Parks said when they reached his office at the rear of the building on the second floor. He opened the door and let Robichaud step inside ahead of him. "Please, take a seat. Can I offer you a coffee, tea?"

"No thanks, I'm good. I don't want to take up much of your time if I can help it," I said.

"Right. The IRA," Parks said, sitting down. "What do you know already?"

"Not a lot. We know about them, of course. We've heard stories that some of their people are here in Halifax but that's it. So far, they haven't done anything to attract our attention. At least, not until now, assuming this is IRA related."

"You are right, of course. There are a few IRA members living here, have been for some time, apparently. Most are connected to their community in Boston. Mostly they are about raising money for The Cause and some gun smuggling."

"Yeah, there's a big Irish community there. Had a few run-ins with them when I was a cop there back in the twenties, but that doesn't explain why they set up here?"

"We think that they are here because of their connections with the Nazis."

"You mean, to spy on the convoys."

Parks nodded.

"Among other things."

"Is that why you indicated that there may also be some German agents operatin' here as well?"

He nodded again.

"I'm guessin' that you don't know where or who these guys are?"

"Well, that's not exactly the case, but then I cannot really discuss this. Sorry. I can say that Cafferty was connected to at least one of these men."

"Okay, I understand. What can you tell me?"

"When we captured him, he told us that there is a network operating here. Their primary function is the acquisition of information on ship movements, cargoes and troop movements. He gave up a couple of names, Sean O'Toole and Iain Kelly, O'Toole being his contact. This Kelly fellow is supposedly running the whole show. We know that Kelly runs a bootlegging house on Inglis Street."

"Yeah, we know about Kelly. So why is he still runnin' loose?" I asked.

"We do not have enough to pick him up," Parks answered.

"We got the same problem. Besides, he's connected at city hall and down on Granville Street, so we gotta be careful goin' after him."

"Can't you take him in as a security risk?"

Parks shook his head.

"Not that simple. When it comes to security you have to understand that it is not as straightforward as it is for the police. He is a link in a complex chain and we do not know either the number of links in that chain or how far it extends. Our job, my job, is to try and learn as much as we can on what each link does and where it connects to."

"Sounds like a tough job and I do understand the importance of security and how it's not a simple matter of one man but a web," I said, "but I don't operate with those concerns. So, where does that leave me in dealing with my current problem? I mean, are your people gonna block me if my investigation takes me to people like Kelly?"

"All I can tell you, Robie, is that I will not interfere in your investigation until such time as it compromises any ongoing security operation."

"What the hell does that mean?"

"It means that if your investigation leads you make certain arrests, we may have to step in and take action. But look on the bright side. If you solve the matter of who actually killed Cafferty, then your case is closed, and if the culprit turns out to be an IRA or German agent, then we will have our hands on someone we can use. We both win."

I sat back, thinking. I knew Parks was making sense. After all, closing the case was really all I wanted to do, but the idea that the killer could get a pass in exchange for turning did not sit well with me. But, this was war. The usual methods and practices did not apply now.

"Okay. I don't like it but I understand. Oh yeah, you should know the paper has already got wind of this. A reporter named Cunningham tried to corner me. But I shut him down for the moment. Might be a good idea for you to give the censor's office a call, get him to lean on the paper until this business is resolved."

"Yes, quite so. I'll make the call," Parks said.

"Now. What can you give me on O'Toole and Kelly?"

Pete Duncan arrived at General Fisheries at Ocean Terminals. He found a place to park, then went in search of the main office. Five minutes later, he was standing in front of a desk outside the plant manager's office. The desk was manned, so to speak, by a very pretty young woman with thick blonde hair and very perky looking breasts under a snug fitting sweater. It was enough for him to crank up his patented charm.

After several minutes of banter, he was told that the manager was away at a meeting with the military and would not likely be back today. He also learned that Marcel LeBlanc worked the graveyard shift, so he wasn't here yet. She said he was likely at home.

He thanked her and, after getting her phone number and accepting his invitation for a date sometime, he headed back to his car and drove over to Bishop Street.

A fortyish looking woman answered the door when he knocked. She carried a few extra pounds but they were distributed nicely over her frame. Must've been a hellava looker twenty years ago, he thought, quickly sizing her up. Force of habit.

"Mrs. LeBlanc?" Duncan asked.

"Yes," she said, with just a trace of a French accent.

"My name is Duncan," he said, showing her his identification. "I'm a detective with the police. Is your husband at home?"

"My husband! Is he in...?" she started to say.

"No, nothing like that. But I need to talk to him about something he saw last night. Is he in?"

"Yes. He's in bed. He works at midnight at the fish plant," she said, stepping back by way of asking him in.

"I hate to bother him like this, but I really need to talk to him. Can you wake him, please?"

"Yes, yes, of course. Please. Go there and sit. I'll wake him." She pointed to a comfortable looking sofa in a small living room as she headed down a short hallway. She returned a few moments later.

"He'll be out in a few minutes. A cup of tea?" she said.

"No thanks, Mrs. LeBlanc. I'm good and won't be here all that long," Pete said.

She left and headed for the kitchen that was across from the living room.

He sat looking around the room. Nice. Warm. Welcoming. She took pride in her home and made the best of what they had. He spotted several black and white photos of a couple of children in brass frames. They appeared to be in their early teens.

She came back a few minutes later with two cups of tea. She placed one on the small table in front of the sofa, then sat in an overstuffed chair. "For my husband."

"Nice looking boys," he said, indicating the photographs.

"Yes. Thank you. That's Pierre and Remy," she said, smiling. "They're in the Sea Cadets."

"That's good. It's a big job."

"Mmm. We all got to do what we can."

Duncan heard a door close and a moment later Marcel LeBlanc stepped into the living room.

He was in his early fifties, still had most of his hair, which at the moment was uncombed. It was black with a generous amount of grey streaking through it. Standing about five eight, he appeared to weigh around 160 or so with a bit of a belly. Must like his beer. He wore a singlet, work trousers held up by a pair of suspenders, and a pair of well worn leather slippers on his feet.

It was obvious that he had been asleep. Duncan stood up and offered LeBlanc his hand.

"Sorry to get you outta bed, but I need to ask you a coupla of questions."

"Sure, I kinda expected to be hearin' from you guys," he said, letting go of Duncan's hand and sitting down on the end of the sofa. He spotted the cup of tea and picked it up.

Duncan sat back down and took out his notebook and pen.

"Okay. Just tell me everythin' you can remember."

"Yeah, right," he said, taking a sip of tea. "I was headin' for work. I'm on the graveyard shift, see. Well, anyway, I'm walkin' along the road an' I see these men, ya know, down at the end of a track between the railcars an' the shed. I thought it was odd. I mean, none of the shed loading doors were open, see. So I'm thinkin' it's somethin' shady, so when I see the beat cop, I tell him."

"And that's all you saw?"

"Uh-huh, that's it," LeBlanc said.

"And you didn't hear anythin'?"

"Hear anything"? Like what?"

"I don't know, maybe talkin' or somethin' else?"

"Naw. No sound. Too noisy anyway. All I knew was what I saw. Them men."

Duncan scribbled in the notebook as LeBlanc talked; his wife sat listening intently but remained quiet.

"What's this all about anyway?" LeBlanc asked.

"Can you remember anythin' about what these men looked like?" Pete asked, ignoring his question.

"Naw, too dark. Just three men for sure. Hey, yeah, wait a sec. I think one of them was holdin' one of the others, ya know, like in a bear hug."

"A bear hug?" Pete asked.

"Yeah, that's what it looked like. I figured it was a shakedown so I took off, you know?"

"Anythin' else?"

LeBlanc shook his head. "Naw, that's it, sorry."

Duncan stood up. "That's, okay. You've been a big help, thanks. We might want to talk to you again. If anythin' else comes to mind call the station. Ask for either Detective Duncan—that's me—or Robichaud. Thanks for your time."

He tore a page from the notebook and wrote a phone number and passed it to LeBlanc.

"Glad to help," he said, standing up and shaking Duncan's hand again.

"By the way, what brought you down to that end of the waterfront. Isn't General the other side of South Street?"

"I was headin' for the canteen. I usually meet up with friends who work with me for a coffee and sandwich before the shift starts."

"Okay, thanks. Hope you can get back to sleep," Duncan said.

"Not a problem," he said as his wife stood and they both led him to the front door.

By the time he arrived back at the office, Robichaud had already returned.

"How'd it go with the navy?" Pete asked, taking off his overcoat and hanging it on a coat peg.

"Not too bad, considering," I said. "You?"

"LeBlanc was at home. Nice enough of a fella. Cooperative, glad to help out. He couldn't add a whole lot more than what MacDonald gave. He did remember two things. There were three men and he's pretty sure that one of the men was holding one of the other two."

"Holding?" I asked.

"Yeah, like in a bear hug, he said. So, whadda we do now?"

"Hmm, fits with what we're thinkin'. As to now, we lay hands on Mr. Sean O'Toole."

"And just how we gonna do that?"

"Pay a visit to Iain Kelly."

"When?"

It was only two o'clock, not that it mattered much, since the bootleggers were operating around the clock these days, especially if the navy and merchant ships were in port. The only plus in going before dark was they wouldn't have to deal with too many drunks...yet.

There was a lot of antagonism toward the military and foreigners in the city, much of it coming out of the church on Tobin Street. The Presbyterians were adamant in their efforts to stop any and every kind of liquor sales in the city and to make matters worse, they were succeeding through their well-established political connections. The only good thing, from the police's point of view, was that, unlike in an American city, Halifax did not have a lot of serious violence beyond brawling and other altercations.

"I think now might be a good time, you know, before the real partiers get started," I said, standing up and reaching for my coat. We pulled our guns from the lockbox, checked them, then put them in our holsters.

"That's what I figured," Duncan said. We headed for the upper parking area.

CHAPTER FIVE

Barrington Street was exceptionally busy with pedestrians, vehicles and lorries. A sign another convoy was being assembled. Most of the shops appeared to be doing a brisk trade despite the shortages.

We eventually made it through the chaos and turned up Inglis Street. Duncan found an empty spot to park up near South Bland and pulled in.

Kelly's place was located on the south side of Inglis Street backing onto Archibald's Coal Plant. The area in front of Kelly's was only moderately busy at this time of the afternoon with sailors and many foreigners from the freighters and tankers anchored in the Basin and harbour, all waiting to get inside to buy a bottle of his rotgut. The real business would start after nine o'clock. We knew he was buying from several moonshiners who ran stills in places like Terrence Bay but couldn't do much about it, even if we had the manpower. The Bay was outside our jurisdiction. It was up to the Mounties to deal with it.

We pushed our way through several men blocking the door.

"Hey, asshole. The line starts back there," a Canadian sailor snarled as we tried to move past him.

I pulled out my identification card and flashed it in the sailor's face.

"I got a free pass," I said.

The sailor looked at the card, then slowly backed up a few steps.

"Okay," I yelled. "Police. Make way."

Like Moses parting the waters, a space suddenly opened up and we walked inside.

"What the fuck you want comin' in here an' messin' with my customers," a man yelled, the Irish accent evident. He stood about halfway up a flight of stairs.

Iain Kelly was a tall man, standing at six foot three. He carried a lot of weight for his height, almost 250 pounds, most of it hard muscle from years on the docks. He had a ruddy face and a seriously receding hairline, which came with age and he was definitely getting up there. I guessed him to be in his early sixties.

"We want to have a talk," I said, starting up the stairs.

"Yeah? 'Bout what?" Kelly said warily. He had dealt with the police before and, even though he was fairly well protected, they could still create problems.

Just then, one of the house bouncers moved in behind Duncan, who turned to face him.

"An' just what do ya think you're plannin' on doin', pal?" he said, stopping the man in his tracks.

"That's okay, Jake. Go on back to da door now. I got this," Kelly said over my head.

The bouncer gave Pete a dirty look, then retreated to his post.

"Good move," Pete said, turning and following me up the stairs.

"Move," I said, pushing Kelly up the stairs.

"Keep yer fuckin' hands off me," Kelly snarled but started up the stairs.

Once inside the room that passed for his office, he went over and sat down on one of three wooden chairs at the old wooden table. He reached for the bottle of Irish whisky that was on it, uncorked it, and poured a large shot into a glass.

"Okay, ya got me alone. Whaddya want?" he said, as he poured. He deliberately didn't offer us a drink.

"We found a friend of yours yesterday. Denny Cafferty." I stood with my hands stuffed into my pant pockets, hooking my overcoat behind my wrists, and watched Kelly carefully for any reaction. Duncan stood at my side casually looking around the room.

"I got a lotta friends. I'm a friendly sorta fella, but I ain't got no friend named Cafferty," Kelly said, taking a pull of the whisky from the glass.

"Funny. We have it on good authority that he and Sean O'Toole are your friends as well as being fellow soldiers in the IRA. You know 'bout the IRA, right? I mean, you're a member yourself I hear."

"No fuckin' idea what yer talkin' about. Me, I'm just a businessman trying ta get by."

"Gettin' by sellin' that piss downstairs to men who're riskin' their lives every day," Duncan said, a hard edge in his voice.

"Hey, ain't gettin' any complaints from anybody."

"We're not here 'bout the quality of your poison," I said, bringing Kelly back to me. "I want to have a talk with O'Toole. Where is he?"

"I don't know any O'Toole."

"So that's the way you wanna play it, yeah? Well, just keep playin' dumb. When we come back knockin' on your door with either the RCMP or the navy boys we'll see how smart you are," Pete said.

"Whadda fuck you talkin' about, RCMP?" Kelly said.

"Well, they're the boys that deal with traitors and spies," I added. "And guess what, asshole? Your buddies in city hall and over on Granville Street won't want to touch ya with a ten foot barge pole once they get wind of what you're really up to."

"You ain't scarin' me none, sure. Unless you got some proof. Then I'll be tellin' ya to get outta my house."

"Okay. You win this round, but we'll be back. And, oh yeah, let O'Toole know we're lookin' for him," I said.

We turned to leave. I paused at the door and, looking back, said, "By the by. Your friend Cafferty is dead with a bullet in the brain. But I'm guessin' you already know that."

"Fuck you." Kelly said to their backs as they left.

"That went well, I'd hafta say," Duncan said when we were back in the car.

"'Bout what I'd expected," I said.

"Whadda we do now?"

"Lay hands on O'Toole."

"Even if we do, then what? We don't have any real leverage we can use on him."

"We got two things."

"Yeah? Enlighten me."

"One. Threaten him with a return to England and a hand over to Special Branch. Two. We still hang people here for murder and treason."

"Jesus. You're one cold bastard, you know that?" Pete said, smiling. "I like that about you."

"I think it's time to give your buddy a call," I said, ignoring the remark.

"Which one? I got so many, ya know."

"Munroe. I think he'd be our best chance at locatin' O'Toole at the moment."

Chet Munroe was a cab driver and a hustler wired into everything that happened in the city's underbelly. Monroe had been a cop until a few years ago when he had to pack it in for health reasons. He took a small pension and bought a used late-model car and was now using it as a taxi with himself as the driver. He made a decent living for himself and his small family.

Munroe was one of those guys that made friends easily and made everyone feel at ease. When he was in uniform he walked a number of beats and over time had acquired a network of contacts. Duncan had become friends with him from when they both joined the force.

"Yeah, okay," Pete said as he manoeuvered the car into the parking area back at city hall.

Pete called the office where Munroe worked out of and arranged for them to let him know he wanted to meet him at the Green Lantern in an hour.

Later, Duncan sat on a stool at the counter of the Green Lantern Canteen eating a toasted sardine and mustard sandwich with a fresh cup of coffee. The place was busy as usual mostly with servicemen and a few civilians. He had placed his coat and hat on the stool next to him, holding it for Munroe.

"Hey, buddy," Munroe said, handing the coat and hat to Duncan, then slid onto the seat.

Duncan took the coat, folded it over, and set it on the counter. "Chet. Thanks for comin' in."

"No sweat. What's up?" Munroe waved at the young girl behind the counter to bring a coffee.

"I'm guessin' you heard about the body some fishermen found the other day."

"Matter a fact, yeah, I heard somethin'. I figured it was jus' some poor bastard got washed over the side or worse," Munroe said as the girl arrived with his coffee, setting it down.

"Anythin' else?" she asked, smiling.

"No, this's good, thanks."

"Yeah, well, it looks like this guy was shot down around Ocean Terminals and his body dumped in the harbour. We think the killer was hopin' it would wash out with the tide," Duncan continued when the girl walked away.

"No shit. And dumped it in the harbour, you say? That had to be no easy task, considerin' how busy everythin' down there is nowadays."

"Yeah, we know. If he did dump the body in the harbour we figure it had to be somewhere out around the Northwest Arm area. Only place outta way enough, with tidal access to open water."

"So whaddya need from me? I'm guessin' it's somethin' to do with this business," Munroe said, taking a sip of coffee.

"Uh-huh," Duncan said. "There's someone we're lookin' for to have a chat. Trouble is, we don't have any idea where he's billeted or hangs out."

"Okay. Gotta name?"

"O'Toole. Sean O'Toole."

"Yeah, seems I heard the name before. Runs a coupla earners somewhere in the northend, I think. Heard he sometimes hangs out down around the Allied Merchantman's Club, you know, down on Hollis. S'ppose to be seeing one of the girls working there. Is he dangerous?"

Duncan shrugged and said, "Don't know. But we believe he's either IRA or connected to them."

"Figures, with a moniker like O'Toole. Say, have you thought about talkin' with Kelly down on Inglis? He's Irish and I hear he's IRA."

"Way ahead of you."

"Not surprised. Robie ain't known to let the grass grow under his feet," Munroe said. "How soon you need this?"

"Yesterday. You got my phone numbers, so call anytime you get somethin'. And, hey, see what ya can dig up on this girlfriend. You know the routine, name, address, that sorta stuff."

"Okay. Guess I'll hit the bricks an' get started. I know a few rocks I can turn over see what's under them." Munroe slid off the stool and headed back to the street.

"Just be careful, hear? Don't take any chances with this guy. Remember, he might be IRA and carryin'. You get somethin', call."

"Don't worry. I ain't no hero. 'Sides, the ole lady have my balls on a clothesline I got hurt."

Duncan couldn't resist a chuckle. He knew his wife and her temper.

He finished his coffee, then settled up with the waitress, including Munroe's coffee. He thought he would take a run down to the Allied Merchantman's Club on Hollis Street. One of the staff there was the chatty type and a regular source for information.

The club was a popular spot for the foreign crews coming into the port. He thought he'd play a hunch that some of these sailors might be Irishmen and that O'Toole, hungry for news from home, might've dropped by. It was a thread, a thin one, but still it might go somewhere with the right pull. Also, he might get lucky and get a lead on this girlfriend.

While Duncan was away meeting with Monroe, I was back at the station. I reached for the phone and dialled, playing a hunch.

"Lieutenant Jolson," the man on the other end said into my ear.

"I figured you'd've wrangled your pension and been on that chicken farm you always harped on about," I said, chuckling.

Frank Jolson was a thirty year veteran of the Boston Police Department. When I first met him, I was just a rookie beat cop and he was a detective in the Bunco Squad at the time, mostly dealing with the illegal gambling that was run by the Irish mob. By the time I quit and left for home, he had made sergeant and was made head of the squad.

"Robie? Dat you?" Jolson said.

"Yep."

"Jesus, boy. It's been a while. Last I heard you was beatin' the bricks back home."

"Not anymore. Now it's Detective Robichaud," I said.

"No shit. Good fer you. Always knew ya had it in ya. So? What's up? I'm guessin' this ain't a 'let's catch up' call."

"Yeah, you're right. I need a bit of help on a case I'm working here might have IRA connections. I remembered that you been workin' that angle back when I was on the force. Figured I'd pick your brain. You know, drop a few names see if any bells start ringin'."

"Mmm. Interestin', but no real surprise. We been hearin' stories that the IRA has sided with the Nazis. No surprise there, what with how they feel 'bout da Brits and given how important yer town is likely to become, makes sense they'd have somethin' goin' on there, I s'ppose. Fill me in on what ya need."

I gave him a broad overview with the lead up to the Irish connection.

"So, what I need from you is, do any of these names mean anythin' to you?" I asked when I finished.

"Matter a fact, yeah," Jolson said, "Iain Kelly."

"How so?"

"Seems he's wired into the IRA cell here and soma da mob guys, mostly for booze an' cigarettes."

"We had our suspicions that he was actin' as a conduit for passin' money and, maybe, even helpin' with their arms traffic. You got any names he's connected to I can use? You know, as leverage?"

"Yeah sure, jus' a sec." I heard the phone drop onto his desk. A moment later he was back.

"Got yer pencil?" he said.

"Yeah, shoot."

"There's Casey Callahan and Michael McDermit, both mob guys, run an operation outta the North End down by da docks. You remember da area. Mostly runnin' a coupla books and cathouses. Branched out a while back to robbery. Rippin' off highway trucks and some traffic offa da docks.

"Next, Liam Clancy. IRA hotshot. Passes as a fundraiser for Da Cause. But we got him down also as big into the arms side a things. 'Cordin' to the feds, he's a suspected shooter too. That's it."

"Thanks, Frank. I'll put this to good use," I said, putting my pen down. "Can you send copies of anythin' you can share?"

"Yeah. No sweat. It'll be in the post tomorrow. Send it special delivery."

I gave him the mailing address.

"Do you know when he last contacted any of these guys?" I heard him shuffling papers.

"Looks like it's been quiet lately. Been, what, six, seven months last we heard from him."

"I suspect it's the war. Too much security. Too many people lookin' and listenin' these days," I said.

"That's probably God's own truth of it. Too bad I can't say it's as quiet here."

"Well, that might change soon if you guys decide to join the party."

"Maybe. But I think I'll be up to my ass in chickens by then. Hey, maybe I'll get a government contract fer fresh eggs and meat. Whaddya think?" Jolson was always going on about how he wanted to pension out and buy a small farm upstate and raise chickens.

"Silver linings, I suppose," I said, chuckling. "Look, thanks again for the information. It helps."

"No sweat. Listen, don't be a stranger. Keep in touch. Ya know, I might be in da market fer a partner. Jus' sayin'."

"Thanks, but I don't think the misses an' kids'd go for it."

"No shit! Ya have been busy."

"Yeah. Livin' here does that to a man."

"Funny how home does that, ain't it. Well, call again if ya need anymore."

I hung up the phone with a wide smile on my face as I remembered my time back then.

Pete had returned about the time I finished talking with Jolson.

"What's with the goofy grin? Sumthin' funny?" he asked as he hung up his coat.

"Huh? No, no. I jus' got off the line with on old friend back in Boston. You might remember me tellin' you about him, Frank Jolson?"

"Yeah, I remember. Likes chickens, right? So, why the call?"

"I remembered that he headed up the squad that covered everythin' to do with the Irish in Boston. I figured I'd have a chat. See what he could tell me about any connections between here and there. Guess what?"

"Shoot."

"Our buddy, Iain Kelly, has direct ties to both the Irish mob and the IRA there."

"We kinda figured there was something, but..." he said.

"Yeah. And now we got some real leverage we can apply," I said.

"Kelly?" Duncan asked.

I nodded.

"I'da thought Parks would be a better bet."

"I think we can work it so he's the anvil. First, we hit Kelly like a hammer by lettin' him know we got his ass in a sling by bringin' him in on smugglin' and racketeerin' charges. Sweat him with the prospect of prosecution and prison time. Then, if that won't loosen his tongue, we use Parks and Special Branch for gunrunnin'. I'd guess that the penalties for that in a time of war would not be very good for continued good health. And, if we're really lucky, we might get us a German agent in the bargain."

"Jesus, you're one devious sonofabitch," Duncan said, smiling. "So when do we spring all this on him?"

"Soon as I get the information from Boston. Jolson's gonna send it special delivery. We'll take it up to Morrison, make sure we got a strong case we can take to the crown prosecutor."

"Man, it'd be great to nail that bastard, shut him down," Pete said.

"You really don't like the guy, do ya?"

"I don't like him makin' money off men puttin' their lives on the line sellin' that poison he calls booze, among other things."

"Yeah. Me too," I said. "By the way, how'd your meeting with Munroe go?"

"Okay. He's on board. Goin' to check out a few places he knows O'Toole frequents. Sez he knows some mates of his who might know where to find him. And, he sez he thinks O'Toole is seein' one of the girls workin' at the Allied Merchantman's Club. Said he'd call if he catches anythin'. I stopped by the club before comin' back to see if my contact there was in. See if he knew anythin', but he wasn't in. I'll go back later."

"Okay. Write it up in the case file. I'm headin' up to fill the boss in on where we are an' get his ideas about Kelly."

I left Duncan to his paperwork and headed upstairs. I knocked on Morrison's door as I turned the knob. As usual, he was sitting behind his desk. This time he was holding his phone against his ear, listening. He looked over and waved me to the chair in front of the desk.

After a few moments, he hung up.

"The Mayor's Office. The navy called. Looks like another big troop movement comin' in soon," he said, sitting back. "Where are you on this Cafferty business?"

"It's movin' along. Still waitin' to get the medical report and the bullet from the VG. Once we have the bullet, it'll be sent to the Mounties' ballistic people. I'm thinkin' it's got to be from one of them special guns, you know, small but with enough kick to do the job, like a .38."

"Hmm, makes sense."

"What I need to talk to you about is somethin' else but related to the case."

"Go on," he said.

"It's lookin' like Cafferty was connected to some sort of IRA activity here, maybe even this German agent Parks referred to. You remember readin' some of the reports with the names of O'Toole and Kelly in them?"

"Yeah. I'm aware of Kelly, not so much this O'Toole. What's the connection?" Morrison asked.

"It's lookin' like Cafferty might've been working with O'Toole, who we are pretty sure is connected with Kelly and the IRA."

"And Kelly?"

"He might be their headman here. I called a friend of mine on the Boston police force I worked with back when I was there. He said Kelly is known to them and that he has definite connections to the local IRA as well as a coupla Irish mob guys. He's sendin' paperwork to me. Should be here next coupla days."

"And you're wonderin' what we can do with the information?"

I nodded, saying, "Yeah, more or less."

"I'm also guessin' you got an idea of how to use it?"

"Yeah, I do," I said, smiling. I outlined my plan in general terms.

"Clever, and workable. Okay, go ahead and hit Kelly with what ya got. I'll call the Crown and see where we stand regarding jurisdiction. Worst case will be that we'll have to pass it over to the Mounties, or intelligence."

"Uh-huh, that's what I thought. By the way, how do you want to handle this with Parks?" I asked. I knew I had to handle the navy carefully.

"Leave him out of it for the moment until I talk to Carmichael over in the Crown's Office."

"Okay, but what if we get a lead on this German before then?"

"Bring it directly to me first."

"Okay," I said, standing up.

"You did good on this one, Robie," Morrison said as he reached for the phone.

"Thanks." I turned and headed back to my office.

Once back at my desk, I called the hospital. They said that they had finished the autopsy and had retrieved the bullet and that everything would be at my office by tomorrow morning. I asked them to forward the bullet over to the Mounties' ballistics lab. My next call was to the lab to give them a heads-up. They said they'd put a rush on running the tests and would send the results as soon as possible.

Since there wasn't a lot to do until everything arrived, I told Pete to clear up and take off early. As for me, I went home to surprise my wife with a little afternoon treat.

Sean O'Toole had a one-room squat in the northend of the city, ironically, not far from Rockhead, the city prison. This was where Kelly and a few others could reach him. He preferred it this way, thinking it was better to steer clear of the part of town that was constantly being watched. However, he also had another place that no one, not even Kelly, knew about. It was a quiet little flat in a private home owned by an elderly widow who didn't ask questions. The flat was rented by Marie Slaunwhite, his woman. She had the place for a while and, in exchange for a minimal rent, she took care of the old woman. Cooking, cleaning, running errands, and such.

He met her at the Allied Merchantman's Club a few months ago where she worked as a server. A nice looker with a decent body, she had come to the city from some fishing hole in Cape Breton looking for work shortly after war was declared. She arrived with enough money to last her a couple of weeks, or so she thought. It didn't take her long to learn the harsh realities of Halifax.

She was a clever girl and quickly learned how to use her sex to get by. Mind, she wasn't working the streets or out of some skanky whorehouse. She was careful and selective in giving herself up to just the right sort who would in turn "help" her out.

That was how he met her.

Late one night, outside the club, a couple of local toughs braced as she left the club. They were pimps running a few women in the area. They didn't like Marie skimming off their trade. Their plan was simple: either force her into working for them or else.

He was coming down the street when he heard her cry out from just inside the alley. He stepped in and assessed the situation, recognising one of the two men. He pulled his pistol and laid it to the side of the nearest man's head, hard enough to crack his skull. When the other one saw him and the gun, he took off at a dead run and, as they say, the rest was history.

He lay propped up against the pillow on the double bed under the window, smoking a cigarette, a glass of whisky on the small side table, an ashtray sitting on his chest.

Things weren't looking good. First, the discovery that Cafferty was picked up by the navy and turned, then the German executing Cafferty without any warning, and finally, his last talk with Kelly.

Maybe it was time for him to get out of the city, maybe head down to Boston. Too many things were happening too fast. The intelligence boys were probably looking for him, especially if Cafferty gave him up. Not to forget the local bulls. They'd be called in and put on his tail. It was also a solid bet that the German had to be thinking the same thing, which meant there was a bullet marked for him. A chill went down his spine at the thought of a gun barrel against his head.

Getting out of the city wouldn't be a problem. He had a plan already in place for just such a situation as this. The problem would be getting away from the German. He figured that Kelly would help him if it came to it, or at least he hoped so. He needed him, especially to set up his arrival in Boston.

Then there was Marie. Would she go with him? Did he really want to take her with him? Could he trust her enough to leave her behind? It wasn't love exactly that made this decision so hard. He knew that they were so good together, better than with any other woman he'd known, and it would be hard to leave her.

Right, he thought, making up his mind. I'll take her with me if she'll come. Okay, he thought. It was time to talk with Kelly, time to make arrangements in Boston.

He swung his feet to the floor and stood up. Five minutes later he was dressed and grabbed his overcoat. He scribbled a quick note for Marie, telling her he'd be back in a couple of hours. Once back outside, he started walking south toward Inglis Street. As he walked the side streets, avoiding the heavy traffic areas where someone might recognise him, he thought living in Boston might work out pretty well, especially if he found a spot with the IRA there.

CHAPTER SIX

The medical examiner's summary report from the hospital arrived at midafternoon the next day. I flipped through it seeing what I expected to see.

Cause of death: single gunshot to the head,
entry point behind victim's right ear at close
range, judging from singed hair around entry
area. Weapon was likely held against victim's skull,
death would have been instantaneous.
No visible signs of any other injuries, offensive
or defensive, indicating victim didn't put up any
resistance. The bullet: small calibre, 40 percent intact.
Sent to RCMP Ballistics as per instructions.

So Cafferty didn't resist. That meant either he didn't see it coming, or, if LeBlanc's account was accurate, someone was holding him when he was shot. A hard way to go, I thought. At least they managed to retrieve the bullet. Hopefully there was enough for the lab to work on, considering how much it must have rattled around inside his head.

The phone rang just as I finished reading.

I put the report down and picked up. "Robichaud."

"Robie. It's Fred at the lab. Just finished with your bullet. Thought I'd give ya a ring before I write it up an' give ya the dime novel version."

Fred Kennedy worked for the RCMP in their ballistics lab.

"That was quick," I said.

"Yeah. Wasn't that hard. There was more than enough to get something. That, and the fact it's a shell you don't see too much around here, if ever."

"Yeah?"

"Looks like it was fired from one of them European manufactured guns, German, I think. My guess would be a Sauer or maybe one of them Italian Berettas, at least that's the closest I found in our reference books. I'd say you lookin' for either a German or one of those foreign sailors been coming here."

"German," I said.

"Yeah? How do ya come to that?"

"We got word there might be a German agent in the area," I said. "Anything else?"

"Not much," Fred said. "But it'd be a good idea to get this gun off the street. It's a nasty piece of work. Soft lead slug with a short powder charge but hard enough to penetrate bone. Does most of its damage once inside. I'd say it's used mostly for in close work like assassinations. I'm guessin' the medical guys didn't like what they saw when they opened up your victim's skull. It spent its energy boucin' around in there. I'll send the report over tomorrow mornin'."

"Thanks, Fred. I appreciate this. I owe ya a beer."

"No sweat. Already put it in the ledger," he said with a chuckle.

"I think you should also send a copy of this upstairs. I'm bettin' they'd be interested."

"Way ahead of ya."

"Thought so. Thanks again," I said, then hung up.

Guess that sort of confirms the shooter was this German agent, I thought, unless the IRA was using a similar weapon, which was a distinct possibility, since they had aligned themselves with the Nazis.

"That the autopsy report?" Pete asked, getting up and coming over.

"Uh-huh." I passed him the one page report.

"That call was from the ballistics lab. Looks like the gun used was likely a German one," I said as he scanned the report.

"German, huh? Guess that sorta confirms Parks's claim 'bout an agent in the city."

"Looks that way."

Pete put the sheet of paper on the desk. "Now what?"

"I better give Parks a call and let him know," I said, reaching for the phone. Pete nodded and went back to his desk.

"Lieutenant Parks," the voice said.

"Michael. It's Robie. Got a minute?"

"Shoot," he said.

"Funny you should say that. I just got the medical report. No real surprises there. Cause of death, a single shot to the head at close range, probably held the gun against his skull. The only interesting item is the shell. According to the RCMP ballistics lab, it's a small calibre soft lead slug. They think it was likely fired from either a Sauer or Beretta. I'm guessin' these are the guns usually used by the Germans."

"Interestin', and, yes, these two pistols are common with their agents."

"How about the IRA? You know if they carry one of the guns?"

"You're wonderin' if it was the German or the Irishman that fired the killing shot, right?"

"Uh-huh," I said.

"Well, from everything we know about the IRA, they usually carry either an American or, more likely, a British made gun. But, given the connection with the Nazis, I don't know for certain. It's possible some may have got their hands on these guns, although our intelligence reports indicate that the Germans are not supplying weapons to them at this time."

"Okay, thanks. That helps," I said.

"No problem. I am interested to hear about the gun though. It's another piece of information confirming the existence of an enemy agent."

"I'll keep you updated as I catch anything that'll help. You want copies of any of this?"

"If you wouldn't mind, thanks," Parks said.

"Okay. I'll have one of our uniforms drop a copy at your reception desk. Talk again soon," I said, then hung up.

Looking over at Pete, I said, "I'm goin' upstairs to see Morrison. Be back in a few minutes."

"Okay," Pete said.

I headed upstairs to brief Morrison on the latest reports.

"So it looks like Parks might be on to something about this agent business," he said when I finished filling him in on the medical and ballistic reports.

"Uh-huh, looks that way, yeah. I called him just before I came up to see you and filled him in on this stuff. I also asked him if he knew if the IRA were known to use these types of guns. He said he didn't think so, since they prefer using either American or British guns, probably because they're easier to get their hands on. Also, there haven't been any reports of the Germans supplyin' them with arms."

"Hmm. So, where's all this leading in your investigation?"

"I'd say it's almost a dead certainty that this German agent is here and he was the one shot Cafferty. Parks did say that these types of guns are commonly carried by the German military and their agents. By the way, where are we with the Crown?" I asked.

Morrison shook his head.

"Nowhere yet. They said this was something they had to get guidance from Ottawa on and the security service people. Out of their realm of experience, as they put it. I understand that. Said they'd call me as soon as they hear anything. What's your next move?" Morrison asked.

"Find and lay hands on O'Toole," I said.

"And Kelly?"

"Not yet. Wanna wait on what the Crown has to say. If he's as big a fish as it looks, then I don't want to do a lot of work until I know I can."

"Makes sense. Okay. Keep me updated."

The meeting was over. I got up and headed back to the squad room. I went over and sat in the empty wooden chair next to Pete's desk.

"So, any luck at the club yesterday?"

Pete sat back and said, "I think so, yeah. Had a chance to chat up one of the staff I know. O'Toole's been hangin' around the club a fair bit lately since he hooked up with one of the girls workin' there. Her name is Marie Slaunwhite. Been working there for a while. She was s'ppose to work last night but didn't show up, so I hung around awhile see if she showed up. She didn't."

"Good work. You get the information on her?" I asked.

"Uh-huh. She's got a place over on Morris Street. No phone."

"Okay. We'll check it out. What about O'Toole? Get anything?"

"Not much more than we already got," Pete said.

"Hear anything from Munroe yet?"

Pete shook his head.

"Nothing in yet from the Crown people?" he asked.

"Nope."

"Shit. I was kinda hopin' we'd be able to haul Kelly in by now."

"Yeah. But we gotta wait. We move too soon, we could blow this case and tip them off."

"Yeah, I know. I jus' hate waitin' is all."

"All part of the job, buddy. All part of the job."

Just then, Carol McIntyre opened the squad room door and leaned in.

She I was a civilian working for the police helping with the clerical side of things, usually helping out on the front desk with the paperwork and filing. Good kid. Eighteen years old and fresh out of high school, quick witted and not too bad looking in the bargain. She wore her light brown hair in a similar style to the actress June Allyson, complete with the barrettes. Guess she thought it made her look older.

"Sorry to interrupt, but there's someone out front wants to talk to a detective."

"Who is it?" I asked, turning around.

"A woman. Mrs. Oakley."

"Did she say what it's about?"

Carol shook her head.

"Uh-uh. Just said she needed to talk to a detective."

"Okay, bring her back."

A few minutes later, Carol escorted Mrs. Oakley into the squad room. I signalled for her to take a seat in the chair at the front of my desk.

"Thanks, Carol," I said as she turned to leave. "Now, Mrs. Oakley, what seems to be the problem."

She wore a woolen tan overcoat and a bandana. The woman looked to be in her forties, a bit on the heavy side, what some would call matronly. Her face had a fresh look without any makeup. She clutched her handbag in both hands on her lap.

"Well, you see, it's about my sister, Clarise. Clarise Halford," she started to say, leaning a little forward and looking a bit nervous.

"Go on."

"Well, I think something might've happened to her."

"What makes you think that?"

"I haven't heard from her for two days now and when I went by her place there was no answer," she said.

"Perhaps she jus' went away somewhere," I suggested.

She shook her head. "No, no, not without telling me. You see, we are very close and talk every day, especially now, with her husband away overseas. He's with the infantry in England."

"Okay, so she's not gone away. Perhaps she's staying with some friends. Have you called around?"

"Yes. I know all her friends and no one has heard from her. I have this horrible feeling something bad has happened to her."

"Okay. Tell me where she lives and I'll send out a patrolman to look into it."

She gave me her address, which I wrote down. She also gave me a photograph of her sister. It had been taken at a beach during the summer and showed her with her sister, both wearing light-coloured summer frocks.

"Is there anything else you can tell me?"

I watched as she lowered her eyes and looked into her lap.

"Is there something?" I pressed.

"I...I don't want to say anything bad about Clarise, but...I think she might've been, you know, unfaithful to Bill. That's her husband. Bill Halford."

"So she could be away with this man, then?"

She shook her again. "No. He boards at her home. He's a foreigner, I think. Anyway, when I went to her house no one was in, not even him."

"Do you have a key to your sister's house?"

"No. I did, but I lost it and haven't gotten around to getting a new one made."

"When you say a foreigner, how do mean? How do know he's a foreigner?"

She shrugged and said, "I can't put a finger on it exactly. He doesn't have an accent but there's just something about him that makes him seem, you know, different."

"Did you happen to get his name?"

"All she told was, Mitchel."

"No first name?"

"No."

"Did she say what he did for work?"

"A welder or something like that, I think."

"And what makes you think your sister might be havin' an affair with this man?"

She blushed slightly at the question.

"Nothing specific, you know, just something another woman would recognise, especially with her sister."

"Hmm. I see." I understood what she meant. My wife had an uncanny sense about things that I've learned not to question. "Well, like I said, I'll have one of our patrols stop by and check out the house and make enquiries. Leave me your contact information and I'll get back to you in a day or two. If your sister should show up, call me so I can call off my men."

She gave me her phone numbers at home and where she worked as well as her address. We stood up and she extended her hand, which I accepted.

"Thank you," she said with a small smile.

I walked her back to the front area. After she left, I spoke with the duty officer and told him to send a patrol car to completely check out the house at the address Mrs. Oakley gave me. I wasn't expecting anything to come of it, but if they did find anything out of the ordinary I told them to report it back to me right away. With all the crap going on these days, I figured it was the least I could do.

"Whaddya think?" Pete asked when I returned.

"Don't know," I said. "Probably jus' a frustrated lonely wife lookin' for some comfort."

"Yeah," he said in a slightly disapproving tone.

"Hey, it ain't easy on those left behind, especially the married ones with no one to talk to, to comfort them and all."

"I know that, but Jesus, he's over there doin' his bit."

"Yeah, an' what if a pretty face offered to comfort him, eh? Think he'd pass?"

"I guess yer right. So, yer gonna take this seriously? You know, her bein' missin'?"

I nodded. "Yeah, an' you know why?"

After a moment or two, Pete snapped his fingers. "The foreigner."

Shortly after lunch, I got a call from the front desk.

"Robie, it's Charlie," the voice said. Charlie Lewis was the duty officer out front.

"What's up," I asked.

"Jus' got a call from that car you wanted me to dispatch. Looks like there's a situation you better go an' look into."

"What is it?"

"One of the uniforms sez he's spotted a woman lying on a bed."

"So? What's odd 'bout that?"

"This one's got a pillow over her face."

"Right. On my way," I said, hanging up.

Looking over at Pete, I said, "Grab yer coat an' let's go."

"What?" he asked, grabbing his coat and hat.

"Looks like we might've found our missin' woman."

"Let me guess, dead?"

I nodded. "Looks that way."

We arrived at the house, which was on King Street in the upper part of the city. It was a small wooden single story structure abutting the sidewalk. The patrol car was parked at the curb. One of the two cops was sitting inside the car while the other stood leaning against the passenger side of the car, bent down slightly as if he was listening.

Pete pulled our car in behind the cruiser and we got out.

"Okay. Whadda we got?" I asked as we approached the cop standing beside the car.

"Me an' my partner were sent to check out this place. We checked the door first. Locked and no answer when we knocked. So we did a walk around, lookin' in the windows. That's when we spotted a body in a bed. That's when Jim there called it in."

"Show us," I said.

He led us down an alley between the two houses to a window at the back. There was a crate sitting under the window. I stepped up and looked in. Sure enough, there was a body lying on a single bed with a pillow over its head. I could also see a naked leg sticking out from under the blanket that partially covered the body. From the shape of it, it was a good bet that it was a woman lying there.

I stepped down and surveyed the back of the house. There was a back door, probably leading into the kitchen, which was usual with this type of house. Pete went and tried the door. Locked.

"Go ahead. Got no choice."

Pete picked up a loose stone lying on the ground nearby and rapped it against the small window in the door. Once he cleared the shards from the frame, he reached inside and opened the door.

"Okay. You two go back to the front and keep anyone away," I said to the two cops before I followed Pete inside. "Oh, yeah. Call dispatch an' have them send an ambulance."

"Yes, sir," one said. Then they turned and headed back down the alley.

Once inside, we headed straight for the room where the body lay. It was a small bedroom, probably converted from a sewing room or pantry. If it wasn't for the war, they might've planned this as a nursery, I thought. It was minimally furnished, just enough to rent out.

I went to the bed where Pete stood looking down. I reached out and eased the blanket off the body. It was a naked woman. Medium build, approximately late thirties, maybe early forties. I glanced quickly at her lower body. I saw a dried crusty looking substance on her inner thigh inches away from her sex. I had a good idea what it was but the medical exam would confirm it. I didn't see any evidence of injury or violence anywhere on her body, so I gently laid the blanket back over her. Next, I pulled the pillow away. Her eyes were open as was her mouth. It also showed signs of her last struggle.

"Poor woman," I said. "Looks like the bastard actually had intercourse with her just before he killed her."

"You think it was the German?" Pete asked, looking away.

"Be my guess, yeah. Looks like this was where he was holed up. Makes sense. Quiet part of the city, away from downtown and any prying eyes. Check out the rest of the house. I'll go through the room here, see if he left anything."

"Okay," he said and left.

I gave the room a thorough look through but, as I expected, found nothing, except for what looked like ashes from a burnt piece of paper. No chance of getting anything from that. I also spotted a loose floorboard in the corner of the closet. I pried it up and checked inside but again found nothing.

Twenty minutes later, we were standing in the front room, watching as the ambulance attendants wheeled the body of Mrs. Clarise Halford out to the waiting wagon. There wasn't anything left for us to do there so we headed for the car. A small crowd, mostly neighbours, had gathered outside. The two uniforms held them back on the opposite sidewalk. I locked up the house and signalled the cops to take off. Pete and I headed back to the station.

I had a call to make that I wasn't looking forward to.

Two days earlier.

Klepp sat on the edge of the bed. He hated the room with its faded wallpaper and aged pictures of people long dead hanging on the wall. It felt and smelled old. A single low watt light set in the ceiling dimly lighted the room. The only furnishings were a four drawer dresser with a wash basin and ewer on top, a small table with a radio on it, and one chrome chair. His single bed was against the wall under the sole window. A crucifix hung on the wall above the pillow.

He sat at a small nightstand with a clean cloth spread over it; a cigarette burned in an ashtray in one corner, a wisp of blue smoke wafting toward the ceiling, and a small lamp on the other corner. Laid out on the cover were the parts of his pistol and a small tin of gun oil. He slowly pulled the wire brush from the barrel of the gun, the bristles sending a fine spray over his fingers as it emerged from the end. He always cleaned the weapon after firing it like he did a few hours ago down on the docks. Ten minutes later, he had reassembled the weapon and, after sliding the cocking mechanism a couple of times and chambering a round, he put it in the leather holster hanging from the back of his chair.

Taking out the bottle of liquor from beneath a folded shirt, he poured out a single shot and downed it all at once. Then he looked at his watch. It was almost time. He went over to the closet and retrieved his well-used suitcase and took it to the bed and opened it.

Making certain the door to his room was locked, he went back to the closet. Kneeling down, he pried two floorboards in a corner and reached inside. He pulled out a medium-sized bundle wrapped in a towel. He stood and went back to the table and removed the towel, exposing a compact radio transmitter receiver and a small leather-bound notebook. He quickly ran a wire from the set to the window, then sat down and placed the earphones on his head. He adjusted a couple of dials and waited for the signal. The set could only be kept open for no more than two minutes to avoid any attempt to triangulate his position.

After a few moments, he heard several beeps in the headphones. Ninety-two seconds later, he tapped his key twice, signalling the message was received, then broke off the connection. He opened the notebook and ran a finger down through the series of letters matching the ones in there with his message. When he finished, he wrapped everything up and returned them to the hiding place in the closet.

He poured himself another drink and then went back to the table to decypher the coded message. Three minutes later he read the message.

Mission compromised
Depart Caribbean station soonest
Terminate Irish contacts
New orders to follow

Interesting, he thought, striking a match and putting the flame to a corner of the paper. Well, at least he was finally getting out of this godforsaken shithole of a city. He sat for a moment wondering what happened to compromise his mission.

His escape plan had already been set up. He would alert the U-boat at the next scheduled contact and arrange for pickup once he finished with his second task—to take care of the Irishmen: Iain Kelly and Sean O'Toole.

Suddenly, there was a soft knock on the door. He instinctively pulled his gun free and stood up, putting his back to the wall.

"Yes?" he called out.

"It's me, Clarise. Are you alone?" a woman's voice sounded from behind the door.

He reholstered the gun and placed his jacket over the chair back, covering the holster.

"Come in," he said, opening the door.

Clarise Halford stood there barefoot, wearing a housecoat. She was in her late thirties, maybe early forties and still fairly attractive. Her husband was overseas with one of the Canadian infantry regiments stationed in England. They did not have any children so she lived alone. She decided to open her home and rented out a room. It didn't take him long to seduce her.

"I thought I heard sounds, so I guessed you were in."

"Sounds?" he said, looking carefully at her.

"Uh-huh. Kind of like beeps or something," she said, going over to the bed and sitting on the edge, letting the housecoat fall open, exposing her legs almost to her pelvis. He noticed she wasn't wearing any underwear.

"Oh, that. It was just my travel clock's alarm," he said, stepping over to her slowly unbuttoning his shirt. Her eyes watched him as he undid them. He saw the hunger in them. When he reached the bed and stood in front of her, she moved her hands up to his belt buckle. A moment later, he felt the cool air on his manhood as it fell free, then the warmth of her lips and mouth.

Thirty minutes later, they were lying naked next to each other, their bodies bathed in perspiration. She lay cuddled tightly against his side, her hand softly stroking him.

It was unfortunate that she heard him on the radio. He could not leave her behind where the authorities might question her about him. What a waste, he thought as he slowly eased himself away from her.

"What's the matter?" she asked softly as she instinctively pulled the bed cover over her nakedness.

"Nothing," he said, bending down and kissing her lightly on the lips. He reached for his pillow and when he broke off the kiss, looked down. Her eyes were closed. Her lips curved in a hint of a smile.

"Come back to bed," she whispered.

He positioned the pillow over her head, driving it down with both hands covering her face, leaning all his weight on the pillow. He looked away as she struggled against the pressure, kicking the bedclothes all over the bed. Within a matter of several moments she succumbed and her legs twitched one last time. Then she was dead.

He stood up and, without a single glance at her body, got dressed, then started to pack up his belongings and the radio, making sure that he left no trace of his having been there. He turned off the light, and closed and locked the door. He headed to the living room downstairs where the only phone was located.

Less than seven minutes later, he hung up the phone, folding the piece of paper with his instructions on it and went out into the street. Luckily, he had made arrangements for an alternative safe house when he arrived. It was on Tobin Street within walking distance of the train station, one of two escape routes. He decided to walk because he did not want anyone noting his movements. Keeping to the shadows and stepping out of sight whenever a vehicle passed, he made it to the new location in forty minutes.

Once he was safely in his new room he started a fire in the small fireplace, which was the only heat source for the room. When the fire was burning high enough, he went over to the cot and lay down.

His first order of business would be to contact the U-boat to stand by to pick him up when he was ready. He closed his eyes and started to outline his plan of action for killing the two Irishmen. It wouldn't be an easy task. These men were not stupid, and they were dangerous, especially, Kelly. He would deal with O'Toole first since Kelly would be the harder target.

CHAPTER SEVEN

"Christ, can you believe this? Two goddamn murders in less than a week," Pete said when we walked into the building from the car park. "This is nuts."

"No kiddin'. I s'ppose we should expect to see more of this shit these days with so many different people comin' into the port," I said.

"Why would that make a difference?"

"A lot of these nationalities don't usually get along like the Greeks and Turks, for example."

"I guess you saw this when you were in the States," Pete asked.

"Uh-huh. That and in the last war."

"I'm guessin' you saw your share of murders when you were in the States too?"

"A few. Never actually worked any of them since I was just a beat cop, but, yeah, I saw a couple."

"So now what? We gonna keep workin' this case or turn it over to the Mounties? We ain't exactly set up to handle a multiple murder case, ya know."

"No goddamn way we're givin' this up. We can manage without them."

Pete raised his hands, "Jus' askin'."

"Sorry. Okay, let's get to it. Whadda we got so far?"

We spent the next ten minutes reviewing what we had to date and speculated on what it meant.

"I think Cafferty was killed because somehow someone found out he was workin' for the Brits and if the ballistics are right, then my guess would be that this German probably killed him."

"I get that, but what about the woman?"

"I think it's a possibility that he also killed her to cover his tracks. That might mean he thinks he's blown his cover and is cleanin' up loose ends before gettin' away."

"Makes sense. Whaddya figure his next move'll be?"

"Well, if what Parks has shared is true, then I'd say he isn't done killin' yet."

"O'Toole and Kelly."

I nodded. "Uh-huh."

"So, whadda we do? I mean, I wouldn't lose any sleep if those two ended up with the fish like Cafferty," Pete said as we entered the squad room.

"I agree, but we're cops an' we gotta do this within the law. Besides, even if he did kill them, we'd have to catch him for the murder of Halford. We owe it to her."

"Yeah, you're right. Okay. How you wanna play it?'

"Well, I'm thinkin' that this guy will probably try for them. I don't know about O'Toole, but I think Kelly will be the more difficult target. So, we have to find O'Toole as fast as we can and bring him in before anything happens. Maybe, if we do, we can squeeze him about the German."

"Okay. I'll get in touch with Monroe. See if he's caught anything yet," Pete said, heading for his desk.

"And let's see if we can find out where this woman of his lives. He might he holed up there," I said, sitting down at my desk.

"Okay."

Five minutes later Pete's phone rang.

"Duncan."

"Pete. I got a call here, sez she wants to talk to ya," the duty officer said.

"Did she say what it's about?"

"Naw, jus' that she wants you. Asked fer ya by name."

"Okay, patch 'er through."

A moment later a woman's voice spoke in my ear.

"Is this Detective Duncan?' she asked, her French accent distinct.

"Yes, I'm Duncan. Who're you?"

"I understand you're looking for me."

"Marie Slaunwhite?" he said, waving at Robie.

"What do you want?"

"We're lookin' for a friend of yours."

"What for?"

"We want to talk to him about someone he knew," Pete said as Robie picked up an extension.

The line went quiet for a moment.

"You still there?"

"Yes. What do you mean...someone he knew?" Pete and Robie both heard the concern and, maybe, even fear in her voice.

"A friend of his was shot the other night down on the docks and we think your friend might be able to help us find the killer and that he might be in danger himself."

The line went quiet again, then, "I'll call you back."

Then the line went dead.

"Now what do you make of that?" Pete said as he hung up.

"Guess we'll hafta wait to find out. But I think this might mean that O'Toole is worried and might be runnin' scared. Either way, we got a chance now to lay our hands on him."

"Ya think he's gonna turn himself in?"

"That, or he's fishin' to see how much we know."

"Think he'd really give himself up? He's IRA after all," Pete said, sounding skeptical.

"Hmm, good point. But maybe he's figured out the German might be gunnin' for him."

"So why don't he jus' run? I'm sure he's got an escape route ready. Maybe down to Boston. They got people there, right?"

"Yeah. It's a puzzle right enough. Maybe it's the woman that's put a wrinkle in his plans."

"Interestin'. Still want me to get in touch with Munroe?"

"Yeah. It'd be good if I could find out where she lives."

"You thinkin' that's where he's holed up?"

"Probably."

"That leaves Kelly."

"Yeah, it does. I think it might be time for another chat," I said. "Maybe he doesn't know 'bout any of this yet. Besides, if he's also a target, then we gotta try an' prevent it."

"Yeah, I s'ppose so," Pete said, standing up and reaching for his coat.

"Hey, if this German takes a run at him in his place that means some innocent people might get hurt."

"Yeah, yer right. Hadn't thought of that, sorry."

"Forget it. Look, I think you should hang around here in case she calls again. I can handle Kelly on my own."

"Okay," Pete said, hanging his coat back on the hook.

The drive down to Inglis Street took a while. Traffic was unusually heavy today with another convoy marshalling for the crossing. This one had several troop transports in it judging by the number of passenger liners tied up at Ocean Terminals.

When I arrived at Kelly's place, I noticed there wasn't the usual crowd lingering out front, again, due to the impending sailing, so I easily made it inside.

We were sitting at the table in his upstairs rooms.

"This gonna become a regular thing with you?" Kelly asked from across the table.

"Not if I can help it," I said. "I'm here to give you a warning."

"Oh, yeah?"

"Yeah. Personally, I'd be jus' as happy to see you go down but then I'd hafta do so much paperwork and it isn't worth the bother."

"Screw you. Get to it so I kin be ridda ya."

"We know that Cafferty and O'Toole are connected to you and that they, in turn, were workin' with a suspected German agent, which means that so were you."

Kelly opened his mouth to say something, but I held up a hand and continued.

"That's the navy's business. My concern is a coupla murders. I got two dead bodies, one is Cafferty with a bullet in his brain and now, a dead woman. I think these two murders were done by your German friend. Now it's jus' possible that this fella is coverin' his tracks before leavin'. Mind you, that's jus' a hunch but not a bad one. And if I'm right, then I'm thinkin' there may be a couple more loose ends he's gonna want to clear up. Whaddya think?" I asked as I studied his reactions.

"Nice story. Got any proof?"

"If I did you'd already be in custody, but then I suppose the proof will be confirmed when we find your body stuffed in a garbage bin or floating out to sea."

"Good imagination. Ya shudda been one a them novelists with a story like that," Kelly said sarcastically. "So why ya tellin' me this?"

I just smiled at him.

"Thought I'd give you a chance to do yourself a favor."

"A favor? How?"

"The German for a twenty-four hour head start to get outta town," I said.

"Assumin' I know this German, which I ain't sayin' I do, why would I do anythin' to help you?"

"You wouldn't be helpin' me. You'd be helpin' yourself. All I'm offerin' is a chance to stay alive and get a free ticket outta here. Remember, I could jus' as easily give all this to the naval intelligence or the RCMP and let them deal with it. Between you an' me, I don't see them bein' so generous, do you?"

Kelly sat there for a moment staring at me, thinking.

"You think yer clever, don't ya."

I didn't say a word. I stood up and looked down at Kelly.

"Think about it. But don't take too long. If I'm right, time isn't on your side."

I left him sitting there and headed back outside. It was getting on to midafternoon when I arrived back at the station. Pete was still at his desk.

"Any word?" I asked, hanging up my coat and hat.

"Yeah. I talked with Munroe," he said, swivelling around in his chair. "Seems our girl has a place somewhere on Morris, which we already know. No one knows a house number."

"That's odd."

"Accordin' to Munroe, she's s'ppose to be really private about herself. Way he hears it, she's been known to put out to certain types for, what'd he call it? Oh yeah, favors. I guess she didn't want people to know where she lived exactly to avoid unnecessary callers."

"Hmm. Did he get a description of her?"

Pete nodded and reached for his notebook, flipping a couple of pages.

"Aroun' five-five. One ten, maybe twenty pounds. Slender build with large breasts. Brown shoulder length hair. Hazel eyes. Speaks with a French accent. Comes from somewhere in Cape Breton, probably aroun' the St. Peter's area. Quiet type. Keeps to herself a lot. No known friends. Arrived in town sometime in the last twelve months. That's it," he said, flipping the notebook shut.

"Okay. Guess we'll hafta do this the old fashion way. Door to door. We'll head out first thing tomorrow."

"Yeah, thought you'd say somethin' like that," he said.

"Look on the bright side. Morris Street isn't that long. We only got to work our way from Lower Water to South Park," I said, reaching for my coat again.

"There's that. How'd your meeting with Kelly go?"

"I left him with somethin' to think about."

"Think he'll roll over?"

I shrugged. "Don't know. He's a tough one and might decide he can deal with the German. Maybe he can. He's got the manpower."

"Let's hope it don't come to that. Otherwise, we might have some more bodies to deal with."

"Speaking of which, anythin' come in on the dead woman?"

"Not yet."

I reached for the phone and dialled.

"It's Detective Robichaud. I'm callin' to see if you have anything on the dead woman, Mrs. Halford," I said to the female who answered the call.

"One moment, please. I'll transfer your call to the medical examiner," she said.

"Thanks."

A moment later a man spoke into my ear.

"Dr. Jefferson speaking. How can I help you, Detective?"

"Has anythin' been done on the Halford case yet?" I asked.

"Only the preliminary findings. I can say with certainty that she died of suffocation. We found traces of fibres and down in her mouth.

Also, there are indications that she had intercourse sometime prior to her death. I will have a more concise report for you by tomorrow."

"Okay, thanks, Doc. That helps. I'll look for the report tomorrow."

"No problem, Detective. Good day," he said, then was gone.

"So?" Pete asked when I returned the phone to the cradle.

"Smothered, probably with that pillow that was over her face. Seems the killer had sex with her before he killed her."

"Jesus, that's one cold bastard," Pete said. "We gotta nail this one, Robie. Nail him hard."

"Yeah. I know."

"You don't sound sure?"

"Don't forget Parks. He'll have a claim on him if we catch him, which means he might walk away from these killings."

"Fuck that," Pete snapped. "I'd shoot the fucker first if I gotta."

"Easy there, Pete. We all got a job to do here. Ours is to catch the bastard and, if we can take him alive, then Parks has a bigger job to do."

Pete looked like he was ready to argue the point, but I raised my hand.

"I don't like it much either, but, like they say, this is a war and we gotta fight it as best we can, so if givin' him up will be to serve a greater cause, then so be it."

"Shit," Pete said as he turned back to his desk.

"You did what?" O'Toole said, looking at her across the table.

"I called the police. They said all they want to do is talk to you. Something about a man being shot down on the docks the other night. A man that was a friend of yours," she said.

"But why'd you call the cops, girl?"

"I'm worried. I know something's wrong and you're scared about something. I just want to make sure you're safe and the detective said that you might be in danger now too."

O'Toole got up and went around to where she sat and squatted down, taking her hands in his.

"There's nothing for you to worry over, pet. Nothing's gonna happen to me, okay? In fact, I've decided it's time to get out of here and I want you to come with me. Whaddya say?"

"Leave? When? Where to?" she asked, looking a bit startled.

"The next coupla days. I got a few things to take of first. As to where, that'd be Boston. I got people there can help set us up. We can start a new life there...together," he said softly.

Marie Slaunwhite stared into his eyes for several moments. "Okay," she whispered. "I have nothing here but you."

He leaned in and kissed her deeply on the mouth as she wrapped her arms around his neck.

He stood up and, lifting her in his arms, carried her into the bedroom as she rested her head on his shoulder.

Iain Kelly was not happy. First, it was Cafferty. He didn't care that he was killed. If he betrayed The Cause he deserved it, but it was a mistake to do the job here. It was guaranteed to draw attention.

Then there was the matter of the German. Was he here with a secret agenda that was a threat to him and the others? Now there was that cop, Robichaud. He braced him here in his place twice in as many days. And now telling him that he should roll over and give up the German, then to get out of town. Did that mean he had something on him? Christ, he thought, reaching for the whisky bottle, this is a mess. He poured a stiff drink and downed it in a single swallow.

He stood and went to the door, opening it.

"George," he yelled down the stairwell.

A moment later, a large burly looking man stepped into view.

"Yeah, boss?"

"No one is to come up 'til I say so, got it? No one."

"Okay." George folded his arms across his chest and stood at the bottom step like a statue.

Kelly closed the door and went back to the table and picked up the phone.

"Yeah?" a man's voice said after five rings.

"It's me, Kelly. I need to talk to Casey."

"Yeah, okay, hang on," the voice said.

Casey Boyen was the head of the IRA's American cell in Boston. He ran everything from there including any activities here in Halifax.

"Iain," Boyen said when he came on line. "Trouble?"

"Aye. Looks that way," Kelly said.

"Talk."

Kelly quickly filled him in on the events of the last couple of days.

"So you see the problem, yeah? Is the German operating under separate orders than we know about and do they include killin' our people?"

"I haven't heard anything about that, but the latest word from Command is that our connection with the Abwehr is getting a bit strained."

"Shite. Whaddya mean, strained? Did this guy get orders to kill Cafferty, then?"

"I don't know. I'll look into it and get back to ya. Now, what about this copper? He gonna be a problem?"

"Yeah, he is. Killin' Cafferty here was a mistake. It ain't like it is in Boston or back home. Killin' ain't a common thing here, so it draws special attention from the cops. Attention we can't afford."

"I know. Can he be bought off ya think?"

"Don't think so. This guy's straight."

"What about takin' him out?"

"Yeah, if necessary, but it'll bring a shitload of grief we don't need."

"Let me think on it a bit."

"You do that. Meantime, what about the German? If he's been given the okay to take us out..."

"Only thing ya can do is cover your ass. Otherwise, we'll hafta give up our operations there. I don't think the Germans would like losin' a valuable source of information from there."

"I get that and I wouldn't be bothered about this except for the killin'. Cafferty was our problem to deal with, not the German's. And now there's been another murder. Some woman. I think Robichaud is maybe connectin' the two to Klepp."

"Was she connected?"

"Don't know."

"Might be a good idea to find out, don't ya think?"

"Yeah, okay. I got someone I can call."

"Right. Let me know when you get anything."

"You too."

"You still have a way out if you need to get away?"

"Yeah, not a problem. Let's hope it don't come to that."

"All right then. Good luck." There was a click in his ear as the line went dead.

Shite, he thought. Boyen didn't sound too worried about what was happening here. Did that mean it was decided that this operation here was no longer of value, and he was no longer needed? He knew how the IRA worked when it came to tying off an operation: no loose ends. Was he a loose end? Was the German the only danger he had to worry about? Should he warn O'Toole? Maybe he could even convince him to take out the German, which would solve two problems at once: remove any threat to him and get Robichaud off his back by providing the cops with the German's body. Maybe.

Reaching for the bottle, he poured another splash of whisky as Robichaud's words came creeping back.

Klepp stood deep inside the shadow of the alley across the street from Kelly's place. Men in uniform, mostly sailors, some army, and a few civilians milled about the entrance. There were also several young women chatting up a few of the men.

There had to be a way to get at Kelly. Outside would be better. He would have the advantage; inside, Kelly did, he thought, as he stood there studying the place. He accepted the fact that if he was to get to Kelly and kill him, it had to be here. Kelly was not known to leave his place that often and seldom with any advance notice. Getting in would not be a problem, he knew. It would be getting out. He also had to assume that Kelly would be cautious and suspicious of him since he shot Cafferty.

He looked at his watch: four ten. He looked across the street again. He had two choices: do it during the day when there were fewer people about, or later, at night, when he could use the crowd to escape the house. Both options presented their own set of risks.

Right, he decided...it will have to be inside. All he had to do was pick the time. Now he had to find and deal with O'Toole. With a quick glance at the house and then the street, he stepped out of the alley and headed down the sidewalk to the corner of Victoria Road. He turned up and made his way to Queen Street, then on to the north end of the city where O'Toole had a room.

Half an hour later, he stood talking to the landlord where O'Toole lived.

"Ain't seen 'im for a coupla days now," he said.

"Look, can you let me into his room? I left some things there and I'm getting ready to head out of town," Klepp said.

"Don't know 'bout that," the man said., scratching his cheek that had a couple of days growth on it.

"You sure you can't help me?" he said, pulling out his wallet and fingering out a five dollar bill.

The old man eyed the bill that Klepp held halfway out of the wallet.

"Well, I s'ppose it wouldn't hurt anythin', you bein' a friend an' all."

Klepp pulled out the bill and handed it to the man, who quickly stuffed it in his pants pocket. He reached inside his room and grabbed a ring with several keys on it and then led the way upstairs, Klepp close behind.

Once he opened the door, Klepp stepped inside. The landlord stayed at the door watching him.

Klepp turned and placed a hand on the door. "I'll be several minutes getting everything so I'll close up when I'm done," he said, standing in front of the man.

"Yeah...well, okay," the landlord said, stepping backward into the hall.

"Thanks," Klepp said, closing the door.

He immediately started searching the room, hoping to find a clue to where O'Toole could possibly be. There wasn't much he knew about him or where he frequented or who his contacts were. The only other place he knew about for certain was the Merchantman's Club. He had gone there once with him. Then he remembered...there was a woman.

Ten minutes later, he finished up and headed back to street. Next stop: the Merchantman's Club.

CHAPTER EIGHT

Sean O'Toole had things to do before he and Marie could take off. They would need money to grubstake them once in the States. Marie said she had several hundred dollars saved up she could bring. He didn't ask how she came by so much. He already knew and didn't care. That was then, not now. He could add another five hundred he had stashed away, plus another three from people who owed him. It would be a good start for them. Now, he had to make arrangements in the States for their arrival. He couldn't just show up. It wasn't the way the IRA worked and they would need a place to stay and, eventually, work, so it wouldn't do to start off by pissing them off.

He knew several people in Boston and New York he could call to set everything up. Question was where to go: Boston or New York? Boston offered more opportunities for work, unfortunately they would more than likely be with the mob, but there were also more Irishmen there. People he knew from home. New York, on the other hand, gave him a better chance of less risky work and a better chance to fade out of view. And there was Marie to consider. She was more than capable of taking care of herself and would manage to get by on her own if necessary.

He ordered another coffee from the girl behind the counter at the Green Lantern Café and took out another Black Cat cigarette, lighting it with a wooden match that he ignited with a flick of his thumbnail. As he inhaled a deep pull of the harsh smoke, he made up his mind: New York.

He needed to let Kelly know that he was leaving but decided to not tell him that he was going to New York, instead letting him think it was Boston. Then he had to make the rounds and collect his debts.

That settled, the first thing he had to do was make their travel arrangements. He decided the best way was by rail to Saint John in New Brunswick, then bus to the US border at Calais, Maine, then on to New York. Marie's papers were in order, so that was one less worry. If everything went as he planned, they would be in New York in three or five days, depending on when he could get seats. The only problem he could see would be the frequent travel restrictions due to military requirements, which had priority over any and all other use of the train.

He finished his coffee and dropped fifty cents on the countertop. Once out on the sidewalk, he headed to the nearest bus stop where he caught a tram heading south down Barrington Street toward the train depot. It was still early. The tram was packed with military and civilian riders but he found a small standing space as a few people got off.

The inside of the station was small compared to the grand stations he had seen in Britain. The main room was done in marble and dark wood and an open high arched ceiling. The floor was covered with rows of wooden benches currently occupied by uniformed men and some civilians. Ticket and baggage offices were on either side of the main entrance. A row of glass doors fitted with brass fixtures lined the right side of the room leading to the loading platforms.

The place was filled with dozens of people sitting waiting for trains and passengers, rail employees scurrying about with handcarts or baggage wagons, and men in uniform carrying duffel bags. Black porters hustled behind some passenger or couple or family hauling their bags. The air was thick with the smell of diesel oil and the drone of so many voices, frequently overshadowed by the public loud speakers announcing arrivals and departures.

O'Toole made his way through the press of bodies to the ticket window with the shortest queue.

"Next," the girl behind the metal grille said as he stepped up. "Destination?"

"Saint John," he said.

"Departure date?"

"Next coupla days. How much for two tickets?"

She opened a large book and slid her finger down to the information he wanted.

"There's a train leaving every Monday, Wednesday, and Friday at eight o'clock in the morning, nothing on the weekends. The fare for coach is fifteen dollars per person. We suggest you book as early as you can before your departure date. The next departure with available seats is tomorrow or you'll have to wait for Monday."

"Okay, thanks. I'll book two for Monday." He reached for his wallet.

She opened the drawer under her counter and pulled out two tickets.

She opened another book. "Names?"

"O'Toole and Slaunwhite. She wrote the names onto the page. "How long is the trip?"

"Five to eight hours, depending on priority traffic demands," she answered, taking his money. After a moment, she passed him the tickets after stamping them. "We recommend packing for a couple of meals since there's no food service on board that particular line. Oh, and have your papers with you in case they are needed. The Mounties and the military have been boarding outgoing trains lately doing spot checks."

"Okay, and thanks again," he said, putting the tickets in his pocket. He stepped out of the line and headed for the exit. Since he was down this end of town, he decided to walk down to Kelly's place on Inglis Street. He needed to talk to him, let him know what he was planning...mostly.

"So. Ya made up your mind, then?" Kelly said after O'Toole finished telling him he was leaving.

"Yeah. It's gettin' too fuckin' hot with the cops and intelligence guys pokin' around, an' that fuckin' Kraut shootin' our people," O'Toole said, picking up the glass of whisky Kelly poured and taking a swallow.

"Yeah. Killin' Cafferty was a big mistake. He was ours ta deal with, not his."

"So, what're you thinkin' 'bout this situation? I mean, we got the peelers lookin' into what we're doin' an' the intelligence guys too. I hear there's a cop named Duncan been askin' around lookin' for me."

"I know. Robichaud, his boss, been here twice now. Both times he dropped yer name. I called Boston ta see if they heard anythin' from back home 'bout a shift in our plans or if there's somethin' changed with the Germans. They're checkin' an' will get back to me. Ya made arrangements yet?"

"Yeah. Train on Monday. Headin' for Boston. I need you to make a coupla calls. Get somethin' set up."

"Okay. In the meantime, I think we gotta do somethin' 'bout Klepp."

"Like what?"

"Killin 'im might be a good idea, I'm thinkin'."

"That's a big step. They'd be okay with that?"

"We talked about it, yeah. They're leavin' it up ta me."

"Shite," O'Toole said, finishing his whisky.

"I think it'd be a good idea. Deals with two problems at once, sure. One. It'd get the cops offa our backs. Givin' them the one shot Cafferty. Two. It'd eliminate the threat to us," Kelly said, picking up the whisky bottle and pouring out another drink in their glasses.

"Makes sense, I s'ppose. Ta," O'Toole said, lifting his glass. "So how you figure to do it?"

"Best would be to set up a meet an' take 'im then."

"You know that if he's gunnin' for us he could turn the setup around on us, right?"

"Why I figure we get a coupla my people to back our play."

"Hmm. Maybe. But Klepp ain't stupid, ya know."

"I know, but what choice is there? It's him or us. So? You up for it?'

O'Toole sat there thinking. There were still three days before he could get out of town and away from Klepp. He knew that the city wasn't that big and Klepp would probably find him quick enough. Kelly was right, but he didn't like being picked to pull the trigger. Shooting the bastard wasn't the problem, it was the risk that he might be the one getting shot. But he also knew that the only way he would be safe was to take Klepp out first.

"Yeah," he finally said.

"Hey, don't be lookin' so worried. Way it looks ta me is we got us an edge, sure."

O'Toole gave him a questioning look.

"He won't know we're on ta him or what's comin'."

"Good point. So when do we do it?"

"Tonight, iff'n yer ready."

"Yeah. I'll be ready. So what ya got in mind?"

They spent the next forty minutes setting up the ambush for later that night.

Kelly would call Klepp and arrange a meeting with him and O'Toole to pass on recently acquired information on the upcoming convoy. He would set up the meeting in the northend near the Rockhead prison at midnight. Kelly would have a couple of his men there a half hour earlier to help take him out if needed and to help get rid of the body. They would dump it in Bedford Basin and let the tide carry it to where the cops could find it. It sounded simple enough.

"Sounds good enough, I s'ppose," O'Toole said.

"Okay. I'm gonna call the bastard now an' set it up. Ya have another drink, meantime."

Kelly got up and left the room leaving O'Toole alone. He was back five minutes later.

"We got a problem," he said, sitting down.

"What?"

"I can't reach 'im. Nobody knows where he's gone to."

O'Toole stood up and reached for his coat.

"Where do ya think yer goin'?"

"I can't jus' sit here waitin'. I'm safer on the street where I got a better chance of seein' the bastard comin'. Besides, I got a few places I can look. Maybe I'll get lucky an' get to him first. If not, then I'll be away 'til this blows over."

"Ya mean after he gets ta me, sure."

"You're better off here than I am for Chrissake. It's like a wee fuckin' fort here with yer men an' all."

Kelly glared at him for a moment, then relented.

"Yeah, yer right. Sorry, mate. Jus' me nerves, I guess. Check in when ya can, okay?"

O'Toole nodded as he took out his pistol and made sure he had a round chambered, then put it back inside his coat.

I was back at the office going over what we had to date on the two murders and discussing ideas with Duncan when the call came in from the guys who checked the crime scenes.

"Robichaud," I said into the phone.

"Robie, it's Ken. I think we got sumthin' you'd be interested in from the room where you found the dead woman."

"Great. We're sorta spinnin' our wheels down here on this one," I said.

"When we went through the room, one a the guys found what looks like a secret stash space under some floorboards in a closet. Looks big enough for an average size suitcase, I'd say. And, whoever was there must've tried to get rid of somethin' by burnin' it. We found ashes look like sheets of paper from a book or tablet."

"No shit. That's great. Get anythin' we can use?"

"Not a lot. He did a pretty thorough job of burnin' everythin', except for a few scraps with some symbols or the like still legible."

"Can you get that down here right away?"

"Figured you'd want it. Ed should just about be there with it."

Sure enough, Ken had no sooner finished talking when Detective Ed Kennedy stepped into the squad room with an envelope in his hand. He came over and dropped it on my desk.

"Here ya go," he said.

"Thanks, Ed."

"Got it," I said into the phone. "Thanks. Send us a copy of your final reports on both scenes when they're ready, okay?"

"Yeah, no sweat. Hope you get enough to catch this prick," Ken said.

"Me too." I hung up as Pete opened the envelope and pulled the contents out onto the desk.

There were two sheets of paper. One was a transcription of the symbols Ken found, the other, a summary of notes on his findings. He commented that he couldn't send the original scraps because the damage to the original page was too great.

Both Pete and I studied the symbols trying to make some sort of sense of them.

"Whaddya think? German?" Pete said sitting back in his seat.

I shook my head. "I don't think so. I've known some Germans from the last war and I don't recognize any of these as part of their language. I think these might be part of some code."

"Hmm, yeah, maybe. I guess that means a call to our buddy, Parks."

"Yeah. If anybody will know what this is it'd be his bunch."

"So, if this is a secret code, then our main suspect for her killin' is definitely the German."

"Looks that way, yeah."

"This guy's got a lot to answer for. Spyin' is one thing. I get that in war. But killin' a woman, that ain't right, 'specially if he's been shaggin' her."

"Probably thought he had to get rid any loose ends that might suggest he's plannin' on leavin'."

"Then we gotta get him before he does."

"That and before any more bodies turn up." Pete gave me a funny look.

"O'Toole and Kelly. The German might see them as loose ends if he's been workin' with them."

"Oh, right. I shoulda figured that out myself."

I reached for the phone and dialled.

"Parks."

"Hi, it's Robie. You got some time to see me?"

"Yes, I think so. Say in an hour?"

"Works for me," I said.

"Care to give me a clue?" Parks asked.

I gave him a quick overview of our findings at the crime scene.

"And you think what you have is a trace of the code our friend is using," he said when I finished.

"Maybe. I'm sorta hopin' your people can tell me. Either way, I figured you want to have this."

"Quite right. See you in an hour. I'll leave word at the entrance so you can come straight up."

"Thanks. See ya in a bit."

Before he left Germany for Canada, Klepp had had a meeting with his controller. At that meeting, he was given his sealed orders, code book, and radio frequencies covering his mission. He was also given a list of contacts living in New York, Montreal, and Halifax. Agents that have been there for more than five years. He was only to contact any of these agents in an emergency.

"Hello," a woman's voice said into his ear through the phone.

"Is Mr. Weeks there?" Klepp said.

"No, sorry. You have the wrong number," she said and hung up.

Klepp looked at his watch, as the second hand swept through thirty seconds. Then he picked up the phone and redialed the same number. The call was picked up on the first ring.

"I need to meet with you," he said.

"One hour in front of the bandstand in the Public Gardens. I will be wearing a carnation in my coat lapel and carrying a strapless grip under my left arm," she said, then hung up again.

An hour later, Klepp stood by the canteen in the Gardens facing the bandstand. He scanned the women walking the path in front of it, and then he saw the carnation.

She was approaching from the duck pond, wending her way through the press of people on the gravelled path.

He guessed her to be in her forties. Average height and build with a shapely figure clearly discernible under the knee length overcoat. She was well dressed and wore a fashionable hat that covered most of her blonde hair. Very attractive, he thought. She carried a strapless leather handbag tucked under her left arm.

He made his way toward the designated meeting spot, arriving just moments before she did.

"We'll talk as we walk," he said, taking her elbow and gently leading her along the path, merging with other couples enjoying the day. Standing beside her, he caught a whiff of her perfume. French. She edged close to him as they walked, giving the impression they were a couple.

"Why have you contacted me?" she asked, smiling. Her English was very good.

"I have a problem. My orders have changed and now I must leave. However, I have a couple of details that need seeing to first. One I can deal with. It's the other one."

"I see."

"I need to find a man. His name is O'Toole. He is connected with the IRA here. He may be hiding out with a woman. I think he may suspect that I'm looking for him. It's possible that he may be trying to leave town."

"IRA?"

"Yes. Is this a problem?"

"No. I have ways to find this man. I assume it is urgent that you get to him quickly?"

"Yes. I plan to leave as soon as this matter is resolved."

"I see. I must ask. Is that business about the dead man the police found floating in the harbour the other day your doing?"

"Yes. He was working for the British."

"And your orders are to shut down this operation here and to eliminate the IRA connection?"

"Yes," Klepp said, casually looking around.

"I see."

She said that he should contact her again in two hours. She should have something for him by then.

When they reached the gate at the northwest corner, they stopped and she leaned forward and kissed him on the cheek, then walked away, turning toward Spring Garden Road.

"See you at home, dear," she said for the benefit of anyone listening.

He stood a moment and watched her walk away, the scent of her perfume still in his nose, feeling slightly...aroused. A moment later, he went through the gate and headed for Jubilee Road, then walked back to his room.

He had to plan his move on Kelly for later tonight.

CHAPTER NINE

I reached naval headquarters and entered the lobby, I was told to go straight up to Parks's office. I opened the door and was met by a very attractive and young woman. She wore a stylish and comfortable looking beige tweed jacket buttoned at the middle. A neatly ironed kneelength grey skirt, and a white blouse buttoned at the neck with a maroon silk scarf tied under the collar.

Her light brown hair, cut shoulder length, was held in place by a set of bone combs on either side. I saw that she wore a pair of hose over a pair of very shapely legs; the black seam running straight from heel to the hem of her skirt. I couldn't quite guess her age, but assumed it was under thirty.

At the moment, she was standing in front of an open file cabinet drawer.

"Hello," I said, thinking it was probably a good thing Pete wasn't here to see her.

"Yes, sir? May I help you?" she said, turning from the drawer, closing it part

way. She sounded very businesslike.

"Detective Robichaud," I said.

"Oh, yes, of course," she said. "Lieutenant Parks is expecting you. Please go right in. May I bring you a cup of coffee or tea?"

"No thanks. I'm good. Won't be here that long," I said, smiling.

I rapped on the glass pane as I turned the doorknob and opened the door.

"Ah, Robie," Parks said, standing up as I entered the office. "Good to see you again. Please, sit. Drink?"

I shook my head and took a seat in front of his desk and pulled the envelope from inside my jacket, passing it across his desk.

"I'm afraid it's only fragments, but there are enough symbols or signs maybe for your cryptology people to work with," I said as he opened the envelope.

Parks took a few moments to eye the two pages.

"I'll send this along, thanks. It might be helpful. I'm not really up on what those people do with this stuff. Good at their job though. So how's the investigation progressing?"

"It's moving along."

I filled him in on what we had and some of our ideas. He was especially interested in my thoughts on the German.

"Does this mean you're close to netting him?"

I shook my head. "Not really. But we're pretty sure he was the one who shot Cafferty. We think he also killed a woman found the other day. He was likely roomin' at her home and somehow they ended up sleeping together. She either knew somethin' specific or he might have just figured she had to go simply because she knew him."

"I see. Cold. But then they are a cold blooded bunch by all accounts, coming out of Europe. So I take it you have a plan to take him, yes?"

"Funny you should ask. One of the reasons I wanted to see you. I know that your interest in taking him has priority over mine. I get that. I don't like it, but I can live with it. Anyway, what I'm thinkin' is, if I'm right about him tyin' off loose ends, then he's gonna want to take out O'Toole and Kelly. If, like I said, my hunch is right, then we might have an opportunity to catch him."

"Go on. I'm with you so far."

"Well, there's not much we can do as far as O'Toole is concerned. Hell, we don't even know where he's hidin' out yet. But, Kelly. That's another story altogether."

"I see where you're going. You think that he will try for Kelly at his place?"

I nodded. "Makes sense. After all, it's a fixed location that would give him control over the area and plenty of opportunities to get at him. He probably knows that Kelly isn't known to venture outside his house too often."

"All good points, but wouldn't he risk getting caught, if not by you, then by Kelly's people?"

"Maybe, but what if he goes in late at night when the place is packed with drunks and others lookin' to buy his rotgut."

"Mmm, maybe. So what have you in mind?"

"I'm thinkin' about sending, say four or six, of our uniforms down there to stake out the area. They'd be dressed in civvies, of course. Me and Pete will be there as well. If the description you say Cafferty gave you is reliable, then we have a good chance of spottin' him."

"Yes, I think this could work. I agree with your assessment that he will probably try for Kelly first. Question is when?"

"Probably in the next coupla days, I'd say. With these two killings, he's probably anxious to get away as soon as possible. I just have to clear this with my boss. I know he'll be okay with it, so I think I'll set up for tonight."

"Do you mind a suggestion?" Parks asked.

"Every little bit helps," I said.

"Well, I was thinking. Kelly's place is usually pretty busy most nights the ships are in port, correct?"

"Uh-huh. Go on."

"Well, I was thinking, if either or both our men show up, it could get a bit, um, messy with so many around, especially if they are military, which likely will be the case, if you follow me."

"Umm. What you got in mind?"

"Perhaps I could arrange with the army and navy police units to coordinate with your people on this, sort of as backup, just in case the crowd becomes a problem. What do you think?"

"You think they'd agree? Now? On short notice?" I asked.

Parks nodded, saying, "I have a confession to make. I contacted the appropriate people and spoke with them, giving them a broad overview of our, ah, problem. They understood and are ready to lend whatever assistance you require."

I gave him a long look.

"Good thinkin'. I was kinda hoping we could set this thing up without havin' to run the risk of a riot."

"So, you are on board, then?"

"Yeah, I'm on board. How you wanna set it up?"

"It's your show. I'll go with whatever you want."

I sat and thought about his offer for a few minutes.

"Okay. Here's what I figure. Get your people to have about a dozen men on standby in the area. They can operate as a flying squad if we need them. And, if we're going to do this, we'd better set up some sorta radio network."

"Not a problem," Parks said, reaching for the phone.

"Have any of them ever worked for or with the police before?"

"No, I don't think so, why? Does that matter?"

"Yeah. We don't operate under the same rules or training as the military, so no weapons, only truncheons and whatever they use to contain a large crowd. It's got to remain a police matter until we catch them. We're the ones authorized to go around armed in the city."

"I agree."

"Look. Maybe you can assign someone to, I don't know, liaise or somethin' along that line. Jus' in case we get lucky an' capture him."

"Yes, that would be acceptable. In fact, I think I know the ideal man for this. Me."

"Yeah, thought you'd want to be in on this. Okay. I'll head back and start the ball rollin'. I'll see ya when ya get there. Go right up to Morrison's office. I'll fill him in," I said standing up.

"Okay, thanks," Parks said as he stood too and offered his hand. "I'll be there, say, sixish."

"Right. I'll let Morrison know."

Just at that a moment, there was a soft rap on the glass. The young Wave stepped halfway in.

"Sorry to interrupt, sir, but there's an urgent call for the detective. It's a Detective Duncan," she said.

"Right. Put it through, will you?" Parks said as he gestured for me to use his phone.

A moment later it rang. I picked up.

"Pete. What's up?'

"Remember Cunningham? Well, we jus' got word from the hospital. Looks like someone did a number on him."

"Okay. I'm just about done here. Meet up with me at the hospital. They say where he's at?"

"Emergency."

"Okay. See you in about fifteen minutes," I said and hung up.

"What happened?" Parks asked.

"A reporter with the *Chronicle*. He tried to talk to me 'bout the Cafferty killin'. Looks like someone jammed him up good. He's in emergency."

"You think he's on to something?"

I shook my head. "No, don't think so. Knowin' him, he probably poked the wrong person and got himself smacked 'round for his trouble."

"Let me know if he's going to be a problem and I'll arrange for a call from Mr. Jefferson."

H.B. Jefferson was the appointed censor by the federal government for the city. He was a noted journalist himself who wrote for the *Halifax Daily Star*.

"Okay. See ya at the station," I said and headed out, thanking the Wave as I walked by.

I arrived in the emergency room of the Victoria General about ten minutes later. The place was busy as usual with a lot of people, mostly drunken military personnel, MPs, shore patrol, and a half dozen or so civilians. Most were here for treatment of cuts and bruises from fights and brawls. I saw a few on gurneys who looked like they fared a whole lot worse.

I went to the nurse's station looking for someone to take me to Cunningham when I heard Pete call out,

"Robie. Over here." He was standing just outside a curtained-off treatment bay.

"Whadda we got?" I asked when I joined him inside the bay.

Cunningham lay on the white-sheeted bed. He looked terrible. His face was bloodied and I saw the signs of a broken nose. His lips on the right side of his mouth were split and bleeding even though a nurse held a gauze cloth over it. Both eyes were swollen almost shut.

A doctor and another nurse stood on one side of the bed, both working quickly to treat the wounds.

"He gonna make it?" I asked.

"Yeah, but he has taken a very severe beating. Lucky for him, he's out cold at the moment so he doesn't have to deal with the pain," the doctor said, flashing a penlight across Cunningham's eyes.

"Okay. We'll get outta your way and leave him to you. If you get a chance, let us know if you get anything, okay?"

"Uh-huh," he said, without looking up. "This guy won't be going anywhere for a couple of days."

Pete and I walked back through the reception area and out the doors leading to our cars.

"What happened?" I asked once we reached my car.

"He was found in an alley on Tower Road by a passerby who called it in to the hospital."

"That it?"

"Yep. That's it."

"Know what he was doing in that area of town?"

Pete shook his head.

"Hmm. Interestin'. Well, we'll hafta wait for him to wake up to get anything."

"Looks that way. How'd the meetin' with Parks go?"

"Let's head back to the squad room before I answer that, okay?"

"See ya there."

Fifteen minutes later we were back at the station sitting in Morrison's office.

"Okay. Get it set up," Morrison said when I finished outlining my plan. "And make sure the men are carrying their revolvers."

"Yes, sir."

"When do you plan to put them in place?"

"I was thinkin' we'd do it in two three-man teams with Pete in charge of one an' me the other. We'll start at ten tonight and go until four in the morning."

"Why not earlier and longer?"

"I'm playin' a hunch that the German will want to use the bigger crowd as a distraction to get in and escape. Kelly's doesn't usually start hitting its stride until around ten and seldom goes longer than three, four o'clock."

"Gotcha. It's your show. Jus' be careful. Don't shoot anybody don't need it. What time did you say Parks was comin' in?"

"Around six. Told him to come up to you."

"Okay. Let the desk know."

It took me about three and a half hours to put the teams together. I had everyone in the squad room for a briefing around seven o'clock. Parks sat in since he was here. He added what he could including what he believed to be the best description of the German he had. I found a city map that I pinned on the wall. I pointed out the locations I wanted men to post themselves in a way that would give them a good view of the street and house as well as one another. When I finished, I suggested that the men get some rest.

The basement was originally intended as a cold cellar. At some time in the past, it had been renovated with plastered walls and a wooden floor; new electrical wiring had been installed feeding the overhead light and a pole lamp in the corner. It was furnished with two cabinets, one had several bottles of liquor and a wooden Crosley radio on it; a large round table with eight wooden chairs around it was positioned under the ceiling light and two well used settees sat against two adjacent walls. The air in the room was thick with the smells of people, booze, and stale smoke.

This was one of a dozen or so gambling dens in the city.

When O'Toole arrived, he saw five men and two women in the room. The men sat around playing cards at the table with partially filled ashtrays, drinks, and money on it. The women sat together on one of the settees, sipping drinks and talking. Except for the overhead light, the rest of the room was in shadow. He stepped up to the table behind one of the players. He recognized the game right off: Seven Card Stud.

He knew two of the men playing. One of them was who he was looking for to collect on a debt.

"Sean, me son," said the man sitting on the opposite side of the table as he stepped into the light's circle. He was holding the deck of cards in his hands.

His name was Charlie Maxwell. Most people just called him, Max.

He owned the house and ran the games, taking a house cut of all the pots. He sometimes sat in on a game if the table was not full, like now. O'Toole played here quite often, mostly because Maxwell had a reputation for running a clean game.

Rumor is that a shark had come to town a while back and tried to hustle his regulars with a dirty deck. Way the story went, the guy would probably never be able to shuffle a deck of cards again.

"Not tonight, thanks. I need to talk with Billy Boy here when the hand's done," O'Toole said, watching the game play out.

"Suit yerself," Maxwell said, passing the next cards to the two players still in on the hand.

The man called Billy lifted the corner of the card Max dealt him with his thumbnail, then folded. He stood up with his glass in hand, looking quickly at Max and then holding the glass up. Max nodded, indicating it was okay to get another drink from his bar.

"Whazzup?" Billy asked as he stepped over to one of the cabinets with the liquor bottles, O'Toole following behind him.

"I'll be needin' you to fish over that one-fifty you owe me," O'Toole said, declining an offer of a drink.

"Jesus, I ain't got that much on me, man."

"I'll be here 'til Monday next. Then I'm away. I'll be needin' it by then."

"I don't know," Billy said, sounding nervous. "I think I kin get my hands on soma it by then."

"All of it, Billy. I ain't fuckin' with ya here. Get it all by Sunday night. I don't wanna hafta get Kelly to collect, if ya get me."

"Okay. Okay, ya don't hafta threaten me. I'm good fer it, fer Chrissake. Ya know that, right?"

"Sunday night. I'll be at the Lantern at ten o'clock. Be there with my money," O'Toole said, giving him a long hard look, then walking away.

"See ya later," Max said from the table when O'Toole reached the door.

"Yeah," O'Toole said without looking back.

"Ya in?" Max called out to Billy.

Back upstairs, O'Toole met Maxwell's wife, Mildred—a big breasted, overweight woman of 50 plus years.

"Got somethin' ya need ta know," she said, stopping him at the door.

"Yeah?"

"There was some man aroun' lookin' fer ya. Askin' questions'bout when we saw ya an' where he could find ya."

"When was this?"

"A coupla hours back."

"Whatcha tell him?"

"Nothin'. Didn't know anythin'."

"Okay. Thanks, Milly. 'Preciate it."

She shrugged, then turned away. He left the house and, once back on the sidewalk, headed off for downtown. He had two more people to see before calling it a day.

He pulled his pistol from inside his coat and placed it in the right pocket, keeping his hand on it. So, Klepp was looking for him. No surprise. He would have to be careful and alert. His best chance of avoiding any real danger was to make sure he stayed where there were a lot of people. He could fade into the crowd and escape if necessary.

Two and a half hours later he finished what he set out to do. He would have all his money by Sunday night. It would then just be a matter of packing everything up and getting Marie and heading down to the station where they would wait, surrounded by lots of people. But for now, he had to figure out where they would be safe enough until Sunday. The only place he could think of was Kelly's. First, though, he had to get word to Marie and work out a plan for them to hook up on Sunday. He would have her meet him at Kelly's on Sunday night where she would stay until the morning. Then the two would head over to the station together. He saw a tram approaching and jumped on at the stop.

O'Toole stood outside the Green Lantern Café with his back against the wall. The sidewalk was jammed with pedestrians going up and down the street, mostly a lot of young servicemen looking for something to do. He checked his watch: just gone four. Taking out a pack of cigarettes, he tapped one out and put it between his lips, then lit it with a match.

Marie was late. Her shift started at four and she was always early. Always. He kept looking left and right, scanning the mob for any sign of her. Wild ideas and thoughts crept into his mind: Had something happened to her? An accident? Had Klepp found out about her?

Suddenly he saw her making her way across the street. He immediately scanned the people on the street behind her for any signs of Klepp. Nothing.

Marie Slaunwhite was almost all the way across the street when she spotted him and waved. He smiled as she wended her way through the press of people on the sidewalk. Once she reached him he grabbed her in a hug.

"Everything all right?" she whispered in his ear. "You look nervous."

"Jus' edgy is all," he said as he released her and stepped back.

She automatically turned her head from side to side, looking for any sign of trouble, danger.

"Relax, girl. There's nothing there. It's jus' me. Tired I guess." O'Toole said, taking her by the arm and heading off south down the street.

Marie stepped up beside him holding on to his arm.

"Where we going?" she asked.

"I'm takin' you to Kelly's place where you'll stay 'til we're ready to get to the train. You'll be safe there."

"Okay but what about my luggage? I left it at the flat."

"Don't worry 'bout it. Gimme your key an' I'll go fetch it an' bring it to Kelly's."

"Okay but it's on the way to Kelly's. Why don't we just stop and get it?" She was right. Her flat was on Morris Street up near South Park but there wasn't a tram line and the street wasn't usually very busy, which would leave them exposed.

"I don't want you outside any longer than necessary," he said.

They jostled and bumped their way through the mob of people until they reached a corner where he led her across the street. They stopped at the bus stop to wait on the next tram, which was due any minute.

O'Toole remained alert but felt less stressed now that she was here with him and they were on the way to a safe place.

I was sitting at my desk eating a cold Spam sandwich that passed for my supper what with rationing these days. Parks was sitting with me pecking away at a sandwich. Guess he wasn't too partial to Spam. Pete Duncan came in carrying a small wooden box.

"The guns and enough ammo for two reloads," he said, setting the box on his desk. "Duty officer out front jus' told me that Monroe called. Sez he's come up with nothin' so far. Sez it's like the Slaunwhite woman jus' disappeared. He can't figure it out," he said.

"Right. Well, we can't sit aroun' waiting on him gettin' a line," I said, glancing at my watch. We still had almost two hours to kill before we set out. "The men are due in soon. What's the latest on Cunningham? We hear anything yet?"

"Yeah as a matter a fact. Call came in from the hospital. He's awake. Looks like he's all right accordin' to the doc. Gonna be laid up awhile though. Guess we could take a run over there and talk to him. See if there's a tie-in to what we're doin'."

"Yeah. Let's go, You wanna tag along?" I asked Parks.

"Thanks, but I think I'll stay here if it's all the same with you. Sort of hold the fort, so to speak."

"Okay. We'll be back in half an hour."

When we arrived at the hospital we were told that Cunningham was sent up to a ward bed where he would stay for a day or two. We went up and found him in a bed, his head and rib cage wrapped in bandages. He was able to talk and told us that he had been jumped by a couple of liquored up servicemen looking for money for more booze. When he said no they piled on him.

Pete asked why he was in that part of town at night. He explained that he was finished for the day and was on his way to see a girl he was dating who lived on Tower Road.

Satisfied the Cunningham beating had nothing to do with the case, we said we were sorry he got beaten up and wished him a quick recovery, then left.

"Well, at least that's not another complication we gotta deal with," Pete said as we left the hospital.

"There's that. Shame though."

"What?"

"I think we're gonna be dealing with a lot more of this sorta thing in the coming months, maybe years."

"Yeah, s'ppose you're right. It'll be tough on the beat cops for sure."

"Uh-huh. Maybe I'll have a chat with Morrison about steppin' up a greater military police presence in the city. Maybe even have one of them patrol with one of ours."

"Sounds good," Pete said, getting in the driver's seat and inserting the key into the ignition.

At eight thirty, all the volunteer officers were sitting and standing around the squad room. Some were smoking cigarettes. Some were chatting quietly among themselves. Pete sat on the corner of his desk next to the box with the weapons. Parks and I stepped into the room and everyone went quiet.

"Right," I said. "First, I want to say thanks for volunteering for this assignment. As I've already indicated, this is primarily a surveillance setup. However, the two men we're lookin' for are hard cases and we're pretty sure one of them has already murdered two people, one a woman, so you'll be armed. One of these men is a suspected member of the IRA, the other a possible German agent. It's the German who is the killer. If at all possible I want to take them alive, understood?"

There was a smattering of Yes sirs and nods from the assembled men.

"Good. Any questions, so far?" No one spoke up.

"Okay. Here's the plan," I said, stepping over to the city map on the wall.

"You'll pair up and take up positions here, here, and here." I pointed at the specified locations. "Three of you along with either Detective Duncan or me, will be on the street mingling in the crowd. So everybody got it? Any questions?" I asked again, ten minutes later.

"Yes, sir," said a young looking man standing near the back.

"Go on."

"I know Kelly's place. It's on my beat. Usually after ten, eleven o'clock, it's pretty busy. Lots of civilians and servicemen hangin' around. Whadda we do if we hafta deal with these two guys with that mob about?"

"We've set up a radio link to here. Lieutenant Parks here will coordinate with the military police and our guys and will have a flying squad ready to assist if needed. He has also put together a simple set of hand signals we'll use to communicate with each other, so see him when we're done here and pay attention to him. Your main job is to make sure that our suspects don't slip away. I want to contain them in the house if possible. So if you do spot someone or something, don't do anythin' to prevent them goin' inside, and let either me or Duncan know, okay?"

"What about comin' out?" the other man asked.

"Detain them. Clear?"

"Yes, sir. Thanks."

"In fact, Pete, you keep in touch with these guys at the back."

"Any more questions?" None. "By the way, has anyone else patrolled that beat, recently or currently?"

One other man raised his hand.

"I had that beat before Walters," he said, glancing quickly at the man who asked the questions.

"How long ago?"

"Two months. I'm now on the beat down near the depot."

"Okay, jus' to be safe you and him pair up and take the position at the rear of the house by the coal yard. Both of you keep an eye open for anyone who might try to enter or exit from the back. Keep to the shadows as much as you can and remember, I want these guys alive, got it?"

One nodded and the other said, "Yes, sir."

"Okay, men step over to Detective Duncan's desk and get your guns, and good luck tonight."

Parks and I stepped off to a corner.

"Everything's set up with your crowd?" I asked.

"Yes," he said, nodding. "There will be three vehicles standing by a couple of blocks away with sufficient men. They will only arrive if called for."

"Good. Let's hope it won't come to that. The last thing I want is a goddamn shoot-out or riot in that crowd."

"Amen to that. Looks like you put together a good plan. I'm impressed."

"Thanks. It wasn't that hard. Most of these men know the city like the back of their hands. They know what to look for and their way around any of the back alleys our guys could use to get inside the house."

"Like I said...it's a good plan," Parks said with a smile. "Now all we need is for our little flies to step into the web."

Meanwhile, O'Toole and Marie Slaunwhite arrived at Kelly's. Business was light this time of day so they had no difficulty getting inside. He led her upstairs to Kelly's private quarters.

"So this is her, huh?" Kelly said when O'Toole closed the door.

"Yeah. Marie, this is Iain Kelly," O'Toole said. "Iain, Marie."

"Welcome," Kelly said, offering her a chair. "Can I get you somethin'?"

"No thank you, I'm good," she said.

"I gotta leave for about half an hour but I'll be back," O'Toole said.

Kelly shot him a quick look.

"Gotta get her things."

"Risky don't ya think?"

"Should be all right for now. It's still daylight an' she lives over on Morris so I should be okay."

"I advise against it but..."

"You sure it's okay us being here for the night?" O'Toole asked, changing the subject.

"Yeah. I got a coupla more men watchin' things. The bastard tries to get in he'll git himself a surprise. Sure," Kelly said. "Listen, I'm thinkin' that it'll be dark in an hour or so. I say wait 'til then before ya go. Be better I think."

"Yeah, ya might be right. Okay. I'll wait. I'll slip out the back and come back in the same way."

"I'll let the boys know. You carryin'?"

O'Toole patted his coat pocket and nodded. He turned and looked at Marie who remained silent while they talked. He saw the worried look on her face.

"It'll be okay, pet. I'll nip out and get yer kit an' be back before ya know it. Iain here will keep ya safe. Jus' stay here an' think about what awaits us once we're away."

CHAPTER TEN

The squad room was mostly empty with only a couple of men lingering around waiting to leave for their assignment. Most of the others had left to get a coffee or have a smoke. Everyone was ready.

I had laid out the plan and divvied the men into two man teams and assigned specific locations for them to take up. We were all to leave at eight thirty and make our way to Inglis Street, arriving at their spots no later than nine fifteen. Everyone was in place by nine twenty.

There were about twenty to thirty men and women milling about the street, some in front of Kelly's place, some making their way inside, others slipping out, a bottle in hand. I spotted a few couples heading into a dark alley, laughing, sharing a bottle. It wasn't hard to figure out what they had in mind. But that wasn't my concern right then, although I began to see why Morrison was concerned about the level of complaints coming in lately from this neighbourhood.

I stayed on the street mingling with the crowd on the sidewalk, keeping an eye on the faces that passed by. I kept well away from the entrance to the house without losing sight of it. It wouldn't do to have one of Kelly's people recognize me and raise the alarm. Pete was working the crowd farther up the street with a view of the coal yards behind Kelly's. Every so often he and I would look to our men for any signal.

It was nearly ten o'clock when I spotted Pete dashing out of sight toward the back of the house. I made my way there from the other end. When I arrived, I saw my men holding a man pinned on the ground. Pete was standing over them with his gun drawn.

When I reached them, Pete looked at me and said, "O'Toole."

The three of them were in between a couple of small piles of coal. I looked down at the man lying face down with one of our men holding him down with his knee on his back. His partner stood to the side with his pistol out.

"Get the fuck offa me ya bastard," O'Toole spat between clenched teeth.

"Shut up," my man said as O'Toole continued to squirm under his weight.

"Good catch, fellas," I said.

"Now what?" Pete asked.

I thought for a moment. I could shackle him and have him taken back to the station or I could take him into Kelly's place and wait for the German and maybe pressure him and Kelly to talk. I quickly rejected that idea, too many chances for complications.

"Can you two handle him and get him back to the station?" I asked, looking at the men.

"Yes, sir. No problem," one of them said.

"Okay, stand him up and pat him down good, and then head over to where our backup is waiting and get one of them to drive you back. Put him in a cell. You better head off that way so you don't draw attention." I pointed away from the house through the coal yard. "Don't let the navy guy know we got him yet."

"Yes, sir," he said as he stood up, pulling O'Toole up with him by his coat collar.

"Pete, you stay here in case the German tries to get in this way. I'll send one of the men from out front to back you up."

"Okay," he said. "One down, one to go."

I made my way back to Inglis Street where I spotted one of our men nearby. I casually walked up to him, taking out a cigarette and asked for a light. As he struck a match, I ordered him to head over to join up with Pete. Then I went back to working the street.

It must have been nearly one o'clock when I heard the woman

scream. It came from down near the corner of Victoria Road. I took off at a run, arriving where a small crowd had gathered in front of an alleyway.

"Make way, make way. Police," I shouted at the backs of the people standing there. They moved aside as I pushed my way through.

I made it to the front of the crowd and saw a woman being held by a young sailor with her face buried in his chest.

"Okay, step back, everybody. Make room. Not you two," I said, pointing to the sailor and woman.

By now several of our men had arrived and began getting the crowd back and the scene under control. I stepped into the alley. About eight feet in, I saw the body of a man lying face down on the ground. When I knelt down I recognized him as one of my men. I quickly placed two fingers on his neck, checking for a pulse. He was still alive. I reached inside my coat and pulled out the walkie-talkie Parks gave me and depressed the button on the side.

"This is Robichaud. I got a man down. I need an ambulance...now. Corner of Victoria Road. Hurry."

There was a brief crackle in my ear, then, "On the way. Over."

I went back to the body and did a quick search, looking for where he was hurt. A moment later I felt the thick, warm stickiness of his blood on my fingers. He had been stabbed in the back on the left side about three inches below his heart.

"Uuuuggggghhh," he groaned softly.

"It's okay, buddy. Jus' take it easy, okay? Help's on the way," I said softly as I gently placed a hand on his shoulder. "You jus' lie still."

Five minutes later I heard the sound of a siren in the distance.

By the time the ambulance arrived and loaded him in back, the street was crawling with my men and uniformed MPs. Pete and I stood off together watching the ambulance head up Victoria Road.

"Sonnofabitch," he muttered. "How do ya figure he knew?"

"My guess, he probably decided not to approach the house directly. Most likely, he came through one of the alleyways back there," I said, indicating the far end of the alley. "That's when he made our man."

I headed back into the alley with Pete following behind.

"Okay, but why attack our guy? He coulda jus' turned away."

"Maybe our man caught wind of him before he could fade back. Besides, are we certain it was him?"

"Whaddya mean? Of course it was him. Had ta be, right? I mean, who else for Chrissake?"

I looked back at the street, surveying the crowd still milling about.

"Yeah, you're right. It was him." We continued to the end of the alley. When we reached the end, we saw it opened onto a courtyard of sorts with access to several other alleyways.

"Guess there's no point to hang around here now," Pete said.

"Yeah. Tell the men to call it a night and go home. Make sure they remember to bring their guns in."

"Okay. At least we got O'Toole."

"Yeah. I can't wait to have a chat with him."

"What about Kelly? Wanna take him in too?"

"Not yet. Let's see what we can squeeze outta O'Toole first."

We returned to the street. I decided to leave the crowd to the MPs and stood my men down, sending them home. Ten minutes later Pete and I headed back to the station. I was too keyed up to go home and needed to take my anger out on someone.

This wasn't going to be a good day for Sean O'Toole.

It was almost two thirty before Pete and I made it back to the station. I told him to get O'Toole and take him to the interrogation room while I went to the washroom to clean off the blood from my hands.

As I left the washroom and headed down the hall to the interrogation room, Parks stepped up beside me.

"Heard you were back," he said, looking at me. "My God, you look awful."

No point in keeping him in the dark, I thought.

"Guess you heard," I said.

"Uh-huh. I was on the radio when you called for the ambulance."

"Looks like I was right. The German showed up. He got away but not before he knifed one of my men," I said testily. "Oh yeah, we did get O'Toole."

"Great news but what about your man? Is he all right?"

I shrugged. "Don't know yet. He's been taken to the hospital. Look. I need to talk with O'Toole before you take over. I still got to close my file. That won't be a problem, will it?"

I saw Parks had picked up on the tone of my voice as he said, "Certainly. I can wait."

We reached the interrogation room. I opened the door and we stepped inside, Parks closing the door behind him.

The room was windowless with only a small square table and three chairs situated under a bright white ceiling light. O'Toole sat on one side, his wrists still manacled. There was a single brown mug and an ashtray on the table. Pete stood leaning against the wall to my right.

I pulled a chair over and sat down. Parks did the same.

"Not your lucky night, is it?" I said.

O'Toole looked from Parks to me with a contemptuous look on his face.

"Right. Let's cut the crap an' git right to it. Whaddya know 'bout Cafferty's body we found in the harbour, an' don't even think about wastin' my time playin' silly buggers with me. I'm not in the mood. I know it was Cafferty and he was a friend of yours."

"Don't know what..." he started to say as I leaned forward and threw a sharp right jab into his face. His head snapped back, a surprised look in his eyes. Blood began to run down his chin from a split lip.

"I told ya, I'm not in the mood for your crap." I sat back down.

O'Toole spit on the floor, then turned back wiping his sleeve across his mouth.

"Let me lay it out for ya. I got a murder to solve. I know you're involved. I know about the German. I know Kelly is involved. You gettin' all this? I'm not interested in the spying shit you're into, jus' the murders. Who shot him? You or your German buddy? Talk. Tell us exactly what went on that night." I noted the flicker in his eyes when I mentioned the German and Kelly.

"Yeah," he said finally, feverishly trying to figure out how he could get out of this.

"Yeah, what?"

"It was the German."

"Okay. Tell us everything you know about him and where we can lay our hands on him."

"I don't know much about him or where he is," O'Toole said.

"Somehow, I don't believe you," I said.

"That's yer problem," he said.

I started to lean forward again and he immediately sat back anticipating another punch. I felt Parks' hand on my forearm.

"That's enough, Robie. You got what you need now let me do my job," Parks said softly as he gently squeezed my arm.

I shot him an angry look but immediately relented and he let go of my arm. I looked back at O'Toole.

"Here's what yer goin' to do. I'm goin' to send for a pen and some paper an' you're goin' to write out exactly what took place that night down on the docks, got it?"

O'Toole just sat glaring at me.

"I said, ya got it?" After a moment, he nodded slightly.

"Pete."

Pete stepped away from the wall and left the room. He returned a few minutes later and placed the notepad and pen on the table in front of O'Toole.

"Whenever you're ready," I said.

He picked up the pen and started to write. Ten minutes later he put the pen down and shoved the pad across the table. I picked it up and read what he wrote. He detailed the meeting and execution of Denny Cafferty and the disposal of the body. He did not include anything specific about the German beyond his participation in the killing, but I didn't care. That was Parks's problem.

"Okay. Now sign it," I said, pushing the statement back at him. He picked up the pen and put it to paper.

"This war is over for you. You're lucky, though. You won't hafta stand trial for murder and end up at the end of the rope, regrettably. You're 'bout to become a guest of the security services," I said, folding the statement and putting it in my pocket.

He looked at me, a puzzled look on his face. Then he looked at Parks. I got the feeling that he figured he was going to be able to trade his information for some sort of deal.

At this point, Parks stood up.

"Sean O'Toole," Parks said in a formal tone of voice. "I am officially taking custody of you under the authority granted me by the Canadian government on charges of espionage and sedition in time of war."

Earlier that evening

Klepp stood inside the phone booth. He reached up and loosened the overhead lightbulb, then lifted the phone from its cradle, dropped a coin into the slot, and dialled.

"Hello," said the woman who answered on the second ring.

"It's me. Do you have anything?" he asked, looking at his watch. He had to time the call to no more than a minute in case the security people were monitoring all public phone lines.

"Yes. Your friend has been located. He is staying with his associate. I know you need to speak to him so you must hurry because he is planning on leaving on Monday morning by train."

"Good, thank you," Klepp said, then hung up.

He looked at his watch again, ten to twelve. Now would be a good time to make his move. Kelly's place would be busy by now, especially since several navy ships had arrived in port throughout the day and the sailors would be ashore looking for amusements.

He pulled out his pistol and eased the breech back, confirming a round was chambered, then took out the suppressor and screwed it into the muzzle. He scanned the street for any sign of danger, then, seeing nothing to cause concern, he screwed the light back in and left the booth.

It was almost one in the morning when he turned down Victoria Road from Tower Road. Early on, after he arrived in Halifax, he made it a point to study the streets of the city, especially the side ones, in case he needed to evade any risk. He made it a point to learn the network of alleyways leading to and from Kelly's place in particular. His plan was simple enough. He would make his way to the back of the house and enter from the back door. But first, he wanted to survey the front for any signs of the police and to see how many people were around.

He made his way part way down Victoria Road toward Inglis Street, keeping to the shadows, taking advantage of the blackout restrictions. When he reached an alley between two three-story houses he slipped inside and walked to the end.

The small courtyard appeared to be empty. He carefully scanned the area for any signs of people or open windows above before moving out of the darkness. He knew this place was sometimes used by some of the men frequenting Kelly's house for their carnal activities with the women who plied their trade on the street.

Satisfied no one was there, he stepped out and crossed over to another alley and stepped inside. About a third of the way down he saw a man standing at the other end out of sight to the street. A sentry? A policeman? He reached inside the sleeve of his coat and extracted a knife with a four inch blade.

He crept slowly forward, then just as the man seemed to sense him there and start to turn, he rushed forward and thrust the blade with all his strength into his back while clamping his free hand over the man's mouth. He felt the man stiffen as the blade sliced its way through the heavy overcoat into his body. A moment later the body went limp and he slowly eased it to the ground, pulling it a bit farther into the alley.

Klepp quickly scanned the entrance area to see if anyone saw what happened—nothing. He quickly wiped the man's blood off the blade on the man's coat, then stood up and made his way back down to the courtyard. He cursed to himself as he went. It was obvious that they knew about him, but how they figured out his plan to eliminate the Irishmen puzzled him. This now became much more dangerous for him.

As he made his way back to Tower Road he tried to reason out who was watching Kelly's place and why. Did they know about him? Were they there to capture him, or the Irishmen? No matter what they were doing there, this complicated matters. He had to be very careful. The smart thing to do was to get away as fast as he could, but he had his orders to eliminate the Irishmen. They knew too much about the German operations here and elsewhere, especially Kelly.

When he emerged back onto Victoria road he heard a siren approaching. Stepping back into the shadow, he instinctively reached for his gun. A few moments later an ambulance sped by followed by a police car. So, he thought, it seems that there was more than a single man involved in the surveillance, judging by how quick they were responding.

Once he was safely back in his room, he took out his bottle of liquor and poured a large drink. He had to think. He needed to work out a new plan. He sat sipping his drink, then all at once an idea came to him.

CHAPTER ELEVEN

I made it into the squad room at four o'clock that afternoon. Duncan still hadn't come in. It was six this morning when Parks left with O'Toole in his custody and Pete and I checked out to catch some much needed sleep. I was exhausted and stressed from the night's work that saw the capture of O'Toole and the knifing of one of my men. I still felt tired, but my wife had always known how to take the edge off of me —thankfully.

The room was relatively busy with uniforms and detectives nearing their respective ends of shift and filing their reports from the day. The phone on my desk rang.

"Robichaud," I said when I picked up.

"Robie, it's me, Pete."

"Where are ya?"

"Hospital. Call came in half an hour ago about Christopher. The guy that was knifed. You weren't in yet so I came up. Anyway, looks like he's gonna make it. His days on the beat are over though."

"That's good news," I said, feeling relieved at the news. I wasn't looking forward to making the call to his wife if it had gone the other way. "How bad is he?"

"Knife sliced up his lung pretty bad and nicked his windpipe as well, accordin' to the doc."

"At least he's alive. That's somethin'. Is he awake? Did ya get a chance to talk to him?"

"Naw. He's been driftin' in and out. They got him doped up pretty good since the surgery. Doc figures maybe in a day, maybe two, we can talk to him."

"Okay. Look, before ya come back go in an' let him know he's still got a job waitin' for him. It might help get him through this."

"Might not do much good sayin' anythin' since he's out of it," Pete said.

"Don't matter. He'll still hear ya so go tell him **an' it** might help him come back quicker. Then git yer ass back here. We still got to find the German before he kills again."

"Okay. See ya in about twenty minutes."

A few minutes after talking with Pete I picked up the phone again and dialled.

"Lieutenant Parks's office," a familiar sweet sounding woman's voice said into my ear.

"Hello. This is Detective Robichaud. Can I speak to the lieutenant?"

"Yes, sir, one moment, please."

A few moments later Parks came on line.

"Robie," he said.

"Michael," I said. "Jus' wanted to check in see if you caught anythin' useful from O'Toole."

"We are still processing him, but we got a few things. Can't really share those unfortunately, but he did confirm the events leading up to Cafferty's killing."

"That's somethin'. By the way, our man that was hurt is gonna pull through. He's finished as a cop though."

"That is wonderful news. Look, maybe I can arrange to get him something here, you know, on a desk or something."

"Thanks, but I'm pretty sure we'll be able to set him up with somethin' here where he can stay on as a cop."

"Okay, but if not, then call me. So, what are your plans now?"

"Find your German. We still want him for the woman and the attack on our man. and we definitely want to get him before any more bodies show up."

"Thought as much. I know that the German is a security matter, but I have spoken with my superiors and they agree that your people probably have the best chance of finding him than ours, so we'll continue to cooperate if that's okay with you."

"Works for me."

"What's your first step?"

"Kelly. I think it's time to bring the hammer down on the sonofabitch. Hard. At the very least, we'll shut him down and run him outta town."

"I agree. Do you need any extra weight like letting him know that he has gotten our attention?"

"Way ahead of ya. That's the hammer."

"I hope I never get on your wrong side. Keep me updated, and good luck," he said with a chuckle, then hung up.

Pete arrived back ten minutes after my call to Parks.

"Whadda we do now'?" he asked, pulling up a chair next to my desk and sitting down without removing his coat and hat.

"Kelly. It's time he got the message he's done here," I said.

"'Bout fuckin' time." He stood up smiling.

I grabbed my hat and coat and we headed upstairs to the parking lot.

The area around Kelly's was fairly quiet, probably because of the incident last night and the presence of MPs and cops still there.

Pete and I made our way into the house. The door is rarely locked. Kelly runs his business twenty-four hours a day. Inside we were stopped by a burly six foot mug who tried to stop us going any farther. That problem was quickly solved by a fast, vicious right hook to his jaw that Pete threw without any warning. The man staggered back a few steps, then his knees buckled and he collapsed in a heap.

"Police business, asshole," Pete said, rubbing his fist.

"Nice," I said as we headed up the flight of stairs.

"Jesus, that was one hard jaw," he said behind me.

When I stepped on the small landing at the top of the stairs, I grabbed the doorknob and opened the door.

Kelly was sitting at the table leaning over an open ledger. There were a few piles of bills of various denominations and a couple of stacked coins. There was another man sitting there with him. They both looked up when I stepped in. The other man made to get up.

"Sit," I ordered, showing him my badge. He stopped halfway up, hesitated a moment, then sat back down.

"What da fuck you...," Kelly started to say, turning in his chair.

I cut him off midsentence. "Iain Kelly, I'm placing you under arrest."

"Fer what?" he spat.

"I'll figure that out between here and the station. Get your coat, then turn around." I pulled out a set of wrist shackles.

"Fuck you. Ya ain't got nothin' on me. Ya can't do this."

"Coat," I said again. Pete took a couple of steps toward him.

He looked like he was going to make it difficult. I took a step closer to him.

"Easy way or hard way, I don't give a shit. Your choice."

He glared at me for a minute, then slowly stood and went to the coat rack and grabbed his coat. I followed behind him and once he had his coat on I grabbed his right wrist and applied the shackle, then put it on the other one.

He looked over his shoulder and said to the other man, "Ya know who ta call."

I took hold of his elbow and steered him out of the room. The man Pete had decked stood at the bottom of the stairs rubbing the side of his face. He stared at Pete, his eyes burning with anger from the humiliation of being sucker punched. It looked for a second like he was going to be a problem, but then he stepped back.

"Next time," he muttered under his breath as we passed in front of him.

"Anytime, buddy boy. Anytime," Pete said.

Suddenly, Kelly lost his footing on a step and tripped forward. I tightened my grip on his arm to catch him. At that instant I heard the two thuds hit the wall. I instinctively pushed Kelly forward and went for my gun, crouching down. Pete heard the same thing and as he turned and caught Kelly who was trying to catch his balance. A second or two later I heard a door open and close.

"Back door," I yelled at Pete who was now down on a knee holding his gun.

He sprang past the man he hit and when he reached the door, pressed himself against the wall and eased it open. As soon as the door started to move two neat little holes appeared about chest high. He didn't hear any shots.

"He's got a silenced gun. I don't know where he is," Pete called out.

I had Kelly down and was shielding him.

"Okay. Forget it. He's probably hiding in the coal yard and we don't have any backup. Let's get to the car and outta here. He isn't gonna do anymore for now."

We piled Kelly into the back of the car. I slid in as well, sitting next to him still holding my gun while Pete took the wheel.

Kelly sat there visibly shaken.

"Guess somebody thinks your use is up," I said. "Somethin' to think about, eh?"

He turned and shot me a look filled with fear, anger, and hate.

"Naval headquarters," I said when the driver turned onto Barrington Street.

"Whaddya mean, naval headquarters?"

Without looking at him I said, "I just figured out a charge."

With Kelly shackled between us, we entered the building and went up to the deck. The armed sailor on duty stepped over, holding his machine gun at the ready behind us, waiting for a signal from the duty officer.

"Lieutenant Parks," I said, holding Kelly's elbow.

The young officer picked up the phone and dialled. He shot a quick glance past us to the sailor and shook his head. We heard him move away.

"Sir, the police are here again. They appear to have a prisoner with them," he said into the phone.

There was a brief pause as he listened.

"Yes, sir, I understand, right away." He replaced the phone on its cradle and waved to another uniformed sailor at another desk, signalling him to come over.

"Johnson, take these gentlemen down to interrogation room B. Stay with them until Lieutenant Parks arrives," the officer said.

"Sir," the rating said as he moved past the desk. "Follow me, please."

Kelly had been uncharacteristically quiet during all this even as we were taken to the basement. I guessed that he was likely assessing his fate at the moment since it looked like he was about to be given over to the security service.

The German had just tried to kill him and it didn't matter how tough you think you are, when you hear a bullet that close to you it scares the shit out of you, unless you are some kind of crazy person. And now he was about to become a prisoner of the security service, I thought happily.

He knew he couldn't rely on his contacts at city hall and at Province House to help him. Dealing with the local cops was one thing, but no one was going to risk their future going against the feds. He was on his own.

I left Kelly shackled and sitting in the windowless room with Pete while I went up to Parks's office. The sailor stepped up behind me as I headed up the stairs. Guess civilians aren't supposed to move around inside the building on their own, I thought.

"Go right in," the young woman sitting at the desk said when I reached Parks's office. "He's expecting you." My escort turned and left, probably heading back to the basement.

"Thanks." I opened the door and stepped inside. I told him what had just happened.

"My God, talk about luck," he said when I finished.

"No shit." I was still a bit shaken by how close those bullets came to me.

"Now what?"

"I got nothin' to actually hold him on. But I'm guessin' you guys could pull a rabbit outta your hats given his connections to the IRA and the German who, I'm willin' to bet the farm, isn't likely to be on his good side about now."

"I think we could work up something."

I smiled. Looked like Kelly's days in Halifax were about to end.

"How's it goin' with O'Toole?"

"He's cracking, I think. I may have reached my limit with him though," Parks said with a hint of a smile.

"Meanin'?"

"We may be transferring him over to the RCMP. They'll inter him until the end of the war, then ship him back to England where he'll end up with Special Branch."

I nodded. "Did he give up anythin' useful on the German?"

"Not much. The German, his name is Carl Duncan by the way, though that could be a cover name has been very cagey. O'Toole doesn't know where he's been living since he's been here. All meetings were arranged by phone calls or through Kelly, I suspect also by phone. He did say that he thought he heard him say that he had another contact here, another German apparently, but he doesn't know who it is."

"Yeah, well, like you've said, that'd be your worry. Right now, I just want to get the bastard out of town and close my case files."

"Well, then, shall we go down and see how bad we can make Mr. Kelly's life?" Parks said, standing up with a file folder in hand.

"Yeah. Let's go," I said, standing as well. On the way down, Parks and I agreed that he would conduct the interview.

When we stepped into the room, Kelly was still sitting there looking sullen. Pete stood off in a corner, leaning against the wall.

"Come on, then. Let's get this bullshit over," Kelly said with a sneer.

Klepp stood just out of sight at the mouth of an alley halfway up the street from Kelly's place. The street was quiet for the time of day. There were a few servicemen and civilians milling about, some off in small groups talking. A few sat on the curb smoking and ignoring everyone, a bottle of beer on the pavement between their feet.

He checked his watch again. Not quite five. If he was going to make a run on Kelly it had to be now. This would be his last chance before getting out of the city. He quickly stepped out and walked across the street, heading for the coal yard in the back. Once there, he made his way to the back of Kelly's house. He checked the door. It wasn't locked. He pulled out his pistol and attached the suppressor to the end of the barrel, then turned the doorknob, pushing the door slowly inward. The hallway was empty. He heard the sounds of a radio and some people talking. Slipping quietly inside, he eased the door closed while holding his weapon out in front of him.

The hall was short, taking only a couple of steps to reach the corner. He crouched against the wall and slowly peeked around the corner.

He saw a large man standing up from the floor, shaking his head and rubbing his jaw, then a moment later he heard sounds coming from upstairs. The man went and stood at the foot of the stairs.

Klepp moved to the other side for a better view of the stairs. That was when he saw a man in a hat and overcoat appear, followed by Kelly and another man a step behind him. They were almost at the bottom. He saw Kelly's arms were behind him, which meant the two men had to be the police.

Everything that happen next, happened in a blur.

Klepp took aim at Kelly's head. It would be an easy shot since he was only fifteen feet away. He squeezed the trigger twice. At that very instant, Kelly stumbled on a step and lurched forward just enough for the two shots to hit the wall beside him.

Klepp cursed to himself and immediately turned and bolted for the door. Outside he ran to one of the nearby stacks of bagged coal and ducked behind one, holding his gun trained on the door.

A moment later he saw the door move and squeezed off two shots in quick succession, hitting the upper portion of the door in a tight group. He waited a few moments for a response. Nothing.

He eased himself away from his cover and started backing away. After several steps with no one showing themselves he turned and dashed deeper into the coal yard before finally cutting across to South Bland Street. He put the gun in his pocket and headed west toward Robie Street. .

He cursed his bad luck as he walked, but being a professional, quickly dispelled any recriminations and started to work out a plan to get out of the city.

He pulled his coat collar up over his cheeks. The weather had turned decidedly bad in the last couple of hours. This would make escaping by boat difficult, not impossible, but very risky. First, he had to contact the U-boat and determine if it could surface. Then he would have to secure a small boat capable of getting him out to the vessel, which would be over five miles offshore. If this was not possible, he had to work out an alternative plan.

It was very likely that the naval intelligence people were now on to him and possibly the local police, he thought as he walked up South Street, so anything he did would have to be done quickly.

He arrived back at his room twenty minutes later. He turned on the radio for the latest weather report and any news on what happened earlier. While he listened, he retrieved his radio and was in the process of setting it up when the announcer came on air with the half-hour news.

He was almost finished and ready to transmit when he heard,

"And now this. The police are asking for the public's help in locating a man for questioning as a witness in a recent robbery."

The announcer then went on to give a fairly good description of him.

"Anyone with any information is asked to call the police department as soon as possible."

"Scheisse," he muttered out loud after the announcer finished. How did they know what he looked like? He was always careful to be as cautious as possible. Of course, he thought. The Halford woman's sister. They must have discovered her body by now and the sister had seen him on several occasions. The robbery reference must be a cover story, he deduced.

As he sat at the radio transmitter and put on the headset, he raced through the last week trying to remember who had seen him that could make the connection between the bulletin and him. But first, he reached out and slowly turned one of the numbered dials, concentrating on the silence in the headset. Then he heard it: a faint signal. The U-boat must have risen enough to expose its antenna.

He quickly started tapping the finger key, sending a rapid series of beeps. After a moment, he stopped and waited. The reply came back a moment later.

Weather deteriorating...cannot risk surfacing...sea's dangerous...will contact again oh four-thirty hours.

Then the contact ended. He tore the sheet of paper from the pad and burned it. He quickly broke down his equipment and returned it to its hiding place.

He glanced at his watch: nine o'clock. He had six and a half hours to avoid capture. This would give him time to try and secure a way to get out to the U-boat.

Pete and I had returned to the station around six. I went upstairs to make my report to Morrison who seemed happy with our results and agreed with my decision to turn Kelly over to Parks, especially since we still had no word back from the Crown attorney's office on the jurisdiction issue.

Back downstairs, I plopped down in my chair feeling tired and old. Pulling an all night shift, dealing with a wounded officer, and damn near getting my head blown off was finally catching up to me. I had been shot at before, a lot actually, during the last dustup, but this was different. This time I wasn't some random target on a battlefield and that was even scarier to think about.

"You okay?" Pete said, coming over with a mug of steaming fresh coffee and sitting down.

"Yeah. Jus' tired, thanks," I answered, reaching for the mug.

"What the boss say?"

"Good work."

"So that's it? We done?"

I took a careful sip of the hot brew before answering, then shook my head.

"Still got to find the German. I don't think Parks and his bunch are gonna be able to pull it off. They don't know the city like us and they don't have the manpower. So we're still in."

"That from Morrison?"

I nodded and said, "Uh-huh, and Parks also asked us to assist."

"Okay. So what's our next move? I mean, we got O'Toole and Kelly, and Cafferty's dead. We're sorta light on havin' any reliable sources to locate the German."

"I know. I'm thinkin' about bringin' in the radio company. Get them to make a public announcement askin' for any information."

"Might work, I guess, but ya think Parks will agree to that? I mean, the German is still a security matter."

"He'll go along with it, especially if I can set it up in a way without exposing him as a spy. He's not the problem. I'm more worried about Bruce Jefferson, the censor, but Parks can help there I think."

"So you think the German's gonna stick around? I mean, he's gotta be thinkin' his cover is blown and not only with the navy but with us by now, right?"

"Actually, I'm sorta hopin' he thinks that because, if he is, I'm guessin' he's got to stay around until dark since he'd figure it'd be too risky movin' around in daylight."

"Makes sense. But if he's plannin' on cuttin' out tonight, wouldn't goin' public be kinda useless?"

"I don't think he's gonna run tonight unless somethin' happens."

"You know somethin' I don't?" Pete asked.

I nodded. "Yeah. There's a weather front movin' in. Due to hit us overnight and hang in for a coupla days."

"That shuts down gettin' away by water but there's still the buses and trains."

"True, but I'm countin' on him keepin' to his MO of stayin' clear of crowded places."

"You been thinkin' about this a while I'm guessin'."

"Just a bit," I said with a smile.

I picked up the phone and made several calls, the first to Parks.

Michael Parks sat listening to Robichaud on the phone. A few minutes after the call he dialled Bruce Jefferson's office.

"Mr. Jefferson, Lieutenant Parks here, naval intelligence. Do you have a moment?" he said into the phone.

"Certainly, Lieutenant," the man on the other end said.

Parks proceeded to outline the details of Robie's plan. Several minutes later, when he finished, Jefferson asked a few quick questions after which he agreed to allow the plan to go ahead.

Parks called Robie back with the approval.

"Great," Robie said. "I've drafted up the message while I was waiting."

He read it into the phone.

"Sounds good. If nothing else, it should put Borden on the defensive now and seriously affect his movements. What can my people do?"

"I was hopin' you'd put some of your men at the bus terminal and railway station along with my people."

"I can do that. When do you plan to start your deployment?"

"Already makin' arrangements. I have limited manpower resources so I have to use my regular patrolmen and a few volunteers."

"I understand. Now, what if he does expose himself and a capture is made? How do we handle that?"

"Not a problem for me, Michael. He's all yours no matter who bags him. I jus' want to close my file on the Halford murder."

"Very good. Do you want my people to contact your officers when they arrive? You know, to coordinate?"

"Sure, okay. Good idea."

"One last point. Weapons."

"In this case, go ahead and arm your guys. I'll clear it with my boss. After all this guy is a killer."

"Right. You going to be in tonight?"

"Yeah, Pete and I are stayin' around until the bastard's caught or dead."

"Okay. I'll stay here and keep control of our side of the operation."

"I'll let you know if we get any response from the radio announcements."

"Okay. Good luck."

I hung up and made the call to the radio station. By seven thirty the radio announcer was broadcasting the German's description over the airwaves about every twenty minutes or so. I hoped that it would garner something useful within the next twenty-four hours.

The endgame had begun.

CHAPTER TWELVE

The first ten calls came in around nine thirty. Most were not useful, one did sound promising. Pete and I went to investigate but it proved to be a false alarm. Turned out to be a merchant sailor from a Norwegian tanker anchored in the Basin on shore leave. We headed back to the station.

"By the way, heard the Slaunwhite woman left town. S'ppose to've gone to Truro or back home," Pete said as he drove.

"Glad to hear they let her go," I said, looking out my window at the busy sidewalk as we made our way through the traffic.

Marie Slaunwhite had been rounded up in the sweep of Kelly's place after we made our arrest. She was in a small room in the garret. One of my men had found her and brought her in for questioning by a detective and one of Parks's people. Guess they were satisfied she knew nothing.

"Yeah," Pete said, then after a moment, "think we'll get him tonight?"

"Don't know. Maybe. He's got to be feeling pressed, so he'll want to get away as fast as he can."

Pete leaned forward a bit and looked skyward. "Looks like you might've called it. Don't look good for gettin' away by sea."

"Uh-huh."

"We got enough men at the station and depot?"

"Hope so. Won't be easy with all the people movin' in and outta the city these days, especially by bus and train. I'm almost hopin' he tries for the sea."

"Why?'

"'Cause there'll be a lot less risk to any innocent civilians if he decides to make a stand," I said.

"Oh, yeah, right. I didn't think of that. Think it'll come to a shoot-out?"

"Maybe. He's a professional spy and he knows there's only a noose or firing squad waitin' for him if he's taken alive. That's after some serious interrogation by the security people."

"If he makes his run by water, where ya figure he'll take off from?"

"I been thinkin' 'bout that too," I said as we neared the turn into our parking area. "My guess would be somewhere close where he can get his hands on a boat with a straight run to open water."

"That leaves the Northwest Arm and Purcell's Cove on up to Herring Cove. Lots a boats with easy access along the shore. All he'd need is a way to get there."

"Easy enough to steal a car and, yeah, you're right about that way. It's a quiet road, especially after dark, and there's probably not a lot of people up that time of night; fishermen get up pretty early. I don't think he'd make a run to Herring Cove. Too far, and he'd hafta chance gettin' past the Redoubt. The battery run regular round the clock patrols as part of their security, so I don't think he'd risk it that far out. If he makes his run to the sea, it'd be from Purcell's Cove or somewhere nearby."

Pete pulled the car into an open space just as the rain started. We made a quick dash for the entrance and then went downstairs to the squad room.

There was a message sitting on my desk.

Call came in after you left from Mr. Calvin Burgess
after you left. Address: 21 Shirley Street. He thinks
the man we're looking for is renting a room in his house.
Sent two patrolmen in a car to check out.

I reached for the phone and keyed in two numbers.

"Duty desk," a man's voice said.

"Robie. What's the latest on that call you messaged me?"

"Nothin' back yet."

"How long they been gone?"

"'Bout ten, fifteen minutes. Should be hearin' somethin' anytime now," he said.

"They in a radio car?"

"Jus' a sec." A moment later, "Yeah. Want me to raise them?"

"Yeah, and then let me know right away what they find out." I hung up.

"What's up?" Pete asked, standing next to my desk.

"Don't know yet. A report from someone named Burgess. Sez he may have rented a room to our guy. Two uniforms are checking it out."

"Where?"

"Shirley Street."

"Jesus, that means he's halfway outta the city if what we talked about jus' now..." Pete said.

"Yeah, I know," I said, interrupting him.

"This Burgess, he own a car?"

"Shit," I said, reaching for the phone again.

"It's me again. You reached that car yet?"

"Not yet."

"When you do tell them to see if Burgess owns a car. Get the plate number and model details. Got it?"

"Yeah, okay," the duty officer said, then hung up.

"Good catch, Pete," I said.

He just nodded. "Coffee?"

"Yeah, thanks."

Five minutes later, my phone rang. It was the duty desk.

"They jus' radioed in. Looks like you got another dead body," he said.

"Jesus Christ," I snapped, standing up. "Tell your men to secure the area. We're on our way and call the hospital. Tell them to send a wagon, and then call the ME to send someone too. By the way, they say if Burgess has a car?"

"They didn't see one."

"Have one of them check with one of the neighbors and get back to me. If he does make sure they get details on the make and plates if possible," I said.

"Right."

I slammed the phone down.

"What?" Pete asked.

"He's just killed someone else."

"Who?"

"Burgess. Looks like Borden musta heard him making his call to us and killed him."

"Goddamn his soul," Pete snapped. "We gonna to check it out?"

I nodded, reaching for the phone. "In a moment. I need to talk to Parks first."

"Parks," he said into my ear when he answered.

"Robie. Looks like your guy has struck again," I said.

"When? Where?"

"Musta been within the last hour. Looks like he had a place up on Shirley Street. Anyway, the owner of the house musta heard our message on the radio and called in. I sent a coupla patrolmen in a car to check it out. They found the body when they arrived and reported back. Pete and I are about to head up there."

"So. You think he's making a run for it?"

"Be my guess. I had them check and see if the caller owned a car. He didn't. So, he's still on foot, but it wouldn't be too hard for him to steal a car, especially in that neighborhood. Quiet. Almost no traffic and with this weather, likely wouldn't be seen."

"Good point. I'll get on the RCMP right away. Maybe they'll nab him on the road. There shouldn't be too much traffic after dark and, as you point out, in this weather."

"Couldn't hurt, but I don't think he'll make a run on the highway," I said.

"I'm listening."

"I got a feeling that he'll try for open water and hook up with a U-boat."

"What leads you to think there's a U-boat?"

"You. A while back you said you suspected that there was a U-boat lurking somewhere offshore gathering intelligence, maybe even in radio contact with this guy, remember?"

"Yes, I seem to recall saying something of the sort. So, if he is planning to get away by water, where do you think he'll take off from?"

"My guess would be somewhere from the Northwest Arm along to Purcell's Cove. Only place where he can steal a boat seaworthy enough for a trip outside the harbour. His only real threat would be getting by the net defences undetected even though he'd be on the seaward side of them."

"Hmm. You're right. I'll contact the port people and the searchlight squadron at Redoubt to coordinate a surveillance of the area. I'll also have a corvette warmed up and ready to go after the U-boat if necessary."

"Okay. Look, can you get over here and do all that? We'll be taking a radio car so if we catch a break we can act pretty quickly and radio in any information you need."

"I'll be there in fifteen minutes," Parks said, then hung up.

I turned to Pete and said, "Let's go." He grabbed his coat and fell in behind me.

The rain was coming down heavily when we turned onto Barrington Street from the parking area. The wind had also kicked up, sending the water splashing onto the windscreen. Our wipers worked to clear the glass enough for Pete to drive. Fortunately, there weren't any pedestrians out and the street had a minimal number of vehicles on it. Even so, it took us almost twenty minutes to arrive at the crime scene.

I spotted the other squad car parked a couple of houses down. One of the patrolmen was standing outside the entrance to the house dressed in a rain-covered slicker. We parked and exited the car.

"Where's your partner?" I asked as I climbed the four steps to the door.

"'Round back," he said.

"Okay. Talk to me."

"We arrived about a half hour ago. The lights were on when we got here so we knocked on the door but got no answer. Brian, that's my partner, he went 'round back to check it out. I went to look in the windows but they were a bit too high to get a clear view. Anyway, Brian musta found the back door open or somethin' 'cause next I know he's openin' the front door and tellin' me to radio in about the dead man inside."

"Okay, thanks. Stay here. There's an ambulance on the way," I said.

"Yes, sir," he said as Pete and I went inside.

The first thing we saw was the body of Mr. Burgess slumped on the floor against the wall under a trail of his blood on the wall where he'd slid down. A wide swath of his blood had pooled on the floor beneath him from the bullet hole in his chest.

I knelt down and rolled him gently to the side. I noted that the bullet had gone clean through. I looked at the wall and saw the small hole where the bullet had embedded itself. I pointed it out to Pete who pulled out his pocket knife and began to dig it out.

I stood up and made my way down the short hall, carefully stepping over the blood. Just past one of the corners, I spotted the spent casing lying on the floor against the bottom of the opposite wall. I picked it up with my pencil and passed it back to Pete who held an envelope open with the mutilated bullet in it.

"Looks like he was standing here when he took the shot," I said, pointing to the corner. "The old man didn't stand a chance."

"Poor bastard," Pete muttered.

"Let's take a look around down there, see if he left anything behind."

We made our way down the hall. The first room on the right was the kitchen. Farther down the hall there were three doors: one on each side and one straight ahead. The ones on the side turned out to be bedrooms. The middle one was the bathroom. Pictures lined the walls of the hall, mostly family photos. There were several of a young man, his son I assumed.

"You take that one. I'll do this one," I said, indicating the room on Pete's right.

My room was furnished with a single bed, a four drawer dresser, writing desk, and chair with a small Philco Bakelite table radio on it and a small lamp. There was also a small closet in the corner. There were also a half dozen framed photos of the same young man I saw in the hall. Most were school photos. Looks like he was an athlete, football and hockey.

I went to the dresser and started pulling drawers. Looks like Borden left in a hurry, leaving behind several shirts and undergarments. I found a small empty travel bag under the bed but not much else.

Just then I heard a commotion coming from the front of the house.

When Pete and I arrived back in the front, we saw one of the patrolmen holding a woman out on the stoop shielding her so she couldn't see the body. She looked about forty-five, soft brown hair and nice face, which at the moment looked very upset.

"What's going on?" she demanded. "Where's my husband?"

"You're Mrs. Burgess?" I asked.

"That's right. Where's...?"

"I'm afraid I have some bad news for you. Your husband has been killed."

"Oh God, no. Oh God. Let me go. I have to see him, please," she pleaded as she struggled to get free of the constable's firm grip.

"I don't think that'd be a good idea," I said softly, placing a hand on her shoulder. "I'm going to ask you to go with this officer who'll take you to his squad car, okay?"

She looked up at me, staring me in the eyes. Tears ran down her face. A pang of sorrow and anger suddenly ran through me. After a moment, she lowered her eyes and sagged against the man's chest. He gently lead her toward the car.

"Stay with her," I said. "I'll be along in a few minutes."

"Yes, sir," he said.

"You. Brian, is it? Go to the kitchen and start a pot for tea. When it's ready take a cup out to the woman," I ordered the other cop.

"Yes, sir," he said, heading for the kitchen. It was at that moment I heard the faint sound of a siren in the distance. The ambulance would be here momentarily.

I went back into the living room.

"You find anything?"

Pete shook his head. "Just what you'd expect for a married couple. You?"

I shook my head. "Some clothes. An empty travel bag. He left in a hurry. Looks like it musta been his son's room at some time."

A few minutes later a man stepped into the living room where we were standing.

"Hi, Doc. Sorry to get ya out on such a rotten night," I said, facing him with my hand out, which he accepted.

"Not a problem," he said, turning his head toward the body out in the hall. "Looks bad."

"Yeah. A single shot to the chest; looks like he took it in the heart," I said as I lead him back into the hall.

"You touch anything?"

"Yeah, sorry. I moved him just enough to see that the shot went right through him. We pulled the slug from the wall. Found a shell casing down in the hall also. It's in there too."

Pete pulled out the envelope with the bullet and passed it to the ME, who looked up and gave me a hard look. I just shrugged.

"Yeah, well, looks like there's no harm done," he said, taking the envelope, then turning back to the body. "Name?"

"Calvin Burgess."

The ambulance pulled up to the house. Two attendants were at the door carrying a stretcher when the cop named Brian pushed past them.

"The duty officer jus' radioed. Wants ya to call in as soon as ya can. Sez it's urgent," he said.

"Thanks. How's the woman doin'?" I asked as I went to the phone.

"Joe sez she looks like she's in shock or somethin'."

I nodded, picking up the phone, and dialled.

"Robie," I said into the mouthpiece.

"Someone called in a few minutes ago to report his car stolen."

"When? Where?"

"Within the last twenty, thirty minutes. Off a side street near Connaught."

"Shit. Is Parks there yet?"

"Yeah. Got in about ten ago. Put him in the squad room."

"Put me through," I said.

"Robie?" Michael said.

"Yeah. Did you hear 'bout the car theft?"

"Yes, just a few minutes ago."

"Looks like he's makin' a run to the water," I said. "Do me a favour and get some of your people to send word up the line to be on the lookout for the car jus' in case I'm wrong an' he's makin' a run outta the province by road."

"Right away. What're you going to do?"

"Pete and I will head for Purcell's Cove. I'll radio in if we find anything."

"Okay. I'll also alert the people at the Redoubt."

"Good idea. Can you send me back to the desk?"

"Uh-huh."

"Sir?" the duty officer said a moment later.

"You get a description of the car?"

"Yes," he said and proceeded to give it to me.

"Okay. Give everything you got to Parks and dispatch two cars to do a careful search of the Arm area along Purcell's Cove Road, and I mean a detailed look, got it?"

"Sir," he said.

"Good. I'll be out on the Purcell's Cove Road area as well so if anything gets called in, no matter how minor, radio me right away. By the way, I'm sendin' your men back with the victim's wife. Make sure she gets handled easy. Pass her along to Parks."

"Yes, sir."

I turned to Pete and said, "Let's go. Looks like he found a car."

Klepp had just put the radio away when he thought he heard the muffled sound of someone talking on the other side of the door. Cracking the door a few inches he heard the landlord's voice from down the hall. He was on the phone telling someone about him.

He stepped away from the door and retrieved his gun, attaching the suppressor, then quietly moved to the door and opened it farther. He moved quietly down the hall, gun in hand. When he reached the corner, he heard the old man speaking to someone on the phone, saying he'd wait for someone to arrive.

Klepp levelled his gun at the old man's back, waiting for him to hang up.

Calvin Burgess, the owner of the house, finished talking and hung up the phone. He turned around to see the man he knew as Carl Borden, standing there with a gun aimed at him.

He had recently decided to open up his house and rented out the bedroom once occupied by his son, who was now serving overseas. He stood staring at the gun in Carl Borden's hand.

"Who were you talking to? Who is coming here?" Klepp demanded, pulling the hammer back. The sound of the click as it set seemed loud in the silence.

"I...I," he started to say.

"Do not lie to me, old man, or I will kill you," Klepp said.

Burgess desperately tried to swallow; his throat felt bone dry as he stared down at the evil-looking weapon. Cold sweat formed on his forehead and started to run down his back, sending an icy chill through his body.

"Speak," Klepp snapped.

"The...the police," Burgess croaked.

"Danke." Klepp squeezed the trigger.

The gun snapped back slightly in his hand and jumped up. The only sound it made a muted *ppphhhtt*.

A small hole appeared in Burgess's chest in the area of his heart. Blood quickly stained and spread across the front of his white shirt. The impact of the round hitting him made him stagger back against the small table where the phone sat, causing it to tip over. Burgess hit the wall and slowly slid to the floor...dead.

Klepp went back to his room. He guessed he had only a few minutes to pack what he needed—radio, codebook, spare ammunition, and a city map. Once he had everything he would need he headed outside and started walking toward the Northwest Arm, running through his options as he walked, mustering all his discipline to stay calm.

Fortunately, he had studied the city's layout before he arrived, so he had a very good idea of possible places to hide and plan alternate escape routes. He decided on the Herring Cove fishing village. It was located about ten miles down the coast. There would be plenty of boats he could use, and it was located outside the harbour defence nets. His only concern would be the patrols sent out from the battery at the Redoubt. If necessary, he could cut off the road and make his way through the woods to Purcell's Cove and steal one of the small fishing boats moored there.

For now, his first priority was to get a car.

Unfortunately, Burgess did not drive, but there were a number of vehicles parked on the street and in several driveways. His problem would be finding one he could break into and hotwire where no one would hear him. Then he needed to secure a boat to take him to open water.

He walked down Jubilee Road toward Connaught Avenue using the darkness created by the rain clouds and the blackout orders. He spotted a car parked on one of the side streets in the shadows under a large tree.

He crossed over, keeping to the shadows and approached the vehicle. No one was out, not unusual for neighbourhoods like this at this time of night. He stepped up to the passenger side and looked in. The door was unlocked, again not unusual. He opened the door and slid inside, quietly closing the door behind him. He moved over behind the wheel on the driver's side, leaving his bag on the seat. The street had a slight grade so he could easily release the hand brake and let the car roll forward. Once he had enough momentum, he would pop the clutch and jump-start the engine. Unfortunately, he could not get enough speed so, reaching under the steering column, he pulled a few wires and, finding the two he needed, started the motor. Ten minutes later, he was at the junction of Herring Cove Road and Purcell's Cove Road.

He drove down the rough road through the rain. His visibility was restricted by the rain and limited beam from the car's headlamps. Checking the speedometer, he saw that he was only averaging about fifteen to twenty miles an hour.

He steered the car carefully up a sloping grade and rounded a bend. Just ahead, he saw the army three quarter-ton truck parked partway across the road. Two men exited the truck when they saw him approaching. They wore helmets and the heavy black oilskin slickers used by the area fishermen. They both carried rifles. One, the driver, took a few steps forward with a hand raised signalling him to stop. The other soldier stepped around the front of the truck, holding his rifle low but ready.

He would have to act quickly, he thought, as he slowed the car to a stop about fifteen feet from the nearest man. Unfortunately for them, they did not have a torch and stood within the dim light from his car's headlights.

He slipped the transmission into neutral and pulled the hand brake. Reaching inside his coat, he pulled out his pistol and held it in his lap, then opened the door. As he eased out, he raised the gun and fired two quick shots at the second man in from of the truck; then instantly shifted his aim slightly and fired twice more at the first man.

Both men fell to the wet road...dead.

Klepp moved quickly to the bodies and without hesitation put a single shot in each man's skull. Next, he put his gun away and then started to haul the bodies back to the cab of their truck. Five minutes later, he was back in his car and heading away from the scene without a backward glance.

CHAPTER THIRTEEN

The rain was still falling, though not as heavily as a while ago. The streets were mostly empty and wet. The wiper blades slapped back and forth, pushing the rain away. We made good time getting to Purcell's Cove Road. The road was a rough ride at the best of times, but now, in the rain, it was going to be slow and bumpy, especially with our headlights covered except for a narrow slit.

"A thought jus' occurred to me. I gotta feelin' that he's not headin' for Purcell's Cove," I said as we neared Melville Cove.

"Yeah. Why's that?" Pete said.

"Well, if it was me, I'd want to get somewhere with lots a boats *and* on the outside of the net patrols and past the Redoubt so that'd mean Herring Cove. Plus, night like this, he'd have a good chance of gettin' past any patrol and there'd be lots of places he could hide."

"So you're thinkin' we should head right to Herring Cove instead?"

"Yeah," I said.

"Makes sense. You're right about the village. I been there before with my dad. It's sheltered an' outta sight an' it's got lots of boats. And like you said, it's on the right side of the nets and the battery. His only real problem would be getting a boat without drawin' attention."

"We got another problem. We don't know when he plans to meet this U-boat. It's even possible he's made contact already," I said, reaching for the handset of the two-way radio.

"Car two calling dispatch, car two calling dispatch," I said into the microphone.

"Dispatch." A voice crackled through our receiver.

"Robichaud here. Who's this? Over."

"Norm. Whaddya need? Over."

"Get Parks for me, will ya? Over."

"Hang on. Over."

A moment later Michael Parks came on line.

"Parks. Over," he said.

"Mike, Robie. Have there been any reports of radio signals in the last ten hours? Over," I said.

"Matter of fact, yes. Our station at Hartland point reported a very brief signal. It wasn't enough to triangulate, but they're certain that it was land-based. Over."

"How long ago? Over."

"A few hours, maybe a bit more. Over."

"Okay. Looks like our man has made contact with the U-boat and is runnin' to meet it. Get on to your people and have them concentrate their efforts offshore. I got a feelin' they have set a specific time for his pick up, and he'll have to send a signal to let them know he's on the way. Over.

"Can do. Where are you now? Over."

"Headin' down Purcell's Cove Road. We're on the way to the Herring Cove. Over."

"Not Purcell's Cove? Over."

"No. I think Herring Cove is his safest bet to get away. Over."

"Okay. I'll dispatch the corvette I had on standby to patrol the entrance. Over."

"By the way, can you get one of the trawlers tied up in the Arm to cover Purcell's Cove jus' in case I'm wrong? Over."

"Good idea. Leave it with me. Good luck. Over."

"Right. I'll check in again when we get to the village. Out," I said, putting the microphone back on its hook.

We were approaching Ferguson's Cove when I spotted the army

three-quarter-ton truck parked on the side of the road. I didn't see any men.

"Pull up here a moment," I said.

Pete eased our car over to the side of the road and stopped ten feet from the front of the vehicle. We sat looking out the window for any sign of life. Suddenly Pete leaned forward and said, "Look there."

I followed his finger, which was pointing at the truck's windscreen. Then I saw it—the outline of two men inside. I grabbed my torch, opened the door, and got out. I went to the driver's door and opened it, shining the light inside.

The body of the driver lay slumped over against the dead body of his partner. I stepped up on the running board and quickly checked the bodies. I spotted the bullet holes in their slickers and the head wounds. I stepped back onto the road, closing the door, and walked back to our car.

"Now what?" Pete asked after I told him what I found.. "Want to report this to the battery?"

I shook my head. "We don't have the time. Looks like he passed here within the last hour or so. Let's go," I said, picking up the microphone again.

"Car two calling dispatch. Car two calling dispatch."

"Dispatch."

"Norm, Robie. Let Parks know that we jus' passed the Redoubt and found one of their patrols with two dead men in it. He'll know what to do. We're on our way to Herring Cove. Should be there in twenty minutes. Out."

We continued on down the road in silence. While Pete paid attention to the road, I pulled my revolver and made sure it was ready, thinking about the two dead young men back in the truck. This bastard wasn't going to get away, I swore to myself, putting the gun back in its holster.

It was close to midnight when we made it to the outskirts of the cove. The area was in complete darkness except for a single road lamp about thirty feet away that cast its light over the dirt road leading down into the cove.

"Okay, slow up," I said when the first couple of houses appeared out of the gloom. We rolled slowly forward, the sound of our tires crunching over the gravel as we entered the village. The rain had let up but it was still dark from the low clouds and the wind was still a bit stiff. There were a couple more low-watt road lamps placed around the area.

"Turn off the lights. Keep an eye open for the stolen car," I said, rolling my window down so I could listen for any sounds. The only sound I could hear was the surf rolling in and crashing up against the rocks at the cove's entrance.

"Right," Pete said, flipping the light switch.

We were inside the village now. I told Pete to stop the car on a low-rising bank. We quietly exited the car, carrying a torch and a gun in each hand.

A cold light mist covered the area adding a chill to the tension we were both feeling. Suddenly a cat dashed out across the road ahead of us from an alley. We both raised our guns but didn't shoot. I heard Pete mutter a curse as he lowered his gun slightly. It was quiet as a graveyard except for the sounds of the waves in the distance. There wasn't a single soul up and about and no lights were on in any of the houses. We made our way down into the cove on either side of the road carefully watching for any sign of movement and the stolen car.

A few minutes later we neared an old wooden bridge that spanned a running brook fed from a nearby small lake. I panned my light across to the other side for anything that might be there. Again, nothing.

"You sure he's come this way?" Pete said in a muffled voice.

I waited a momen then nodded, gesturing with my gun to start across.

On the other side, Pete moved a few feet ahead of me. He stopped suddenly and crouched down. I immediately dropped to a knee at the end of the bridge.

"Whaddya got?" I whispered.

"I think I found the car," Pete answered.

I moved across to where he was, staying low with my eyes on the area ahead of us.

"Where?"

Pete raised his light and the beam fell on the trunk of a dark-coloured sedan, lighting up its licence plate. It was the stolen car all right.

"Guess you called it," Pete said over his shoulder. "Now what?"

I took a few minutes to consider the situation.

Borden had to be in the area somewhere, but where? Had he already gone down into the cove and secured a boat? Or, did he head to the point so he could radio the U-boat? I was faced with making a choice: split up and send Pete to check the point while I checked the boats, or stay together and risk missing him.

I opted to stay together. This guy was extremely dangerous and not afraid to shoot to kill. I also decided we'd make for the cove. I reasoned that he'd need a boat first and foremost. Plus he could radio from it once he was clear of the cove.

"Okay. Here's the plan. We head down to the boats together," I said.

"Works for me," Pete said.

"Good. Let's go. Stay with me."

We turned to the right and made our way over the rocky dirt road. Our path took us past houses on the left and fish sheds on our right. Looking down, I saw that there were only a few boats actually tied to roughly made log-and-plank piers laden with lobster traps and barrels of nets.

"Which one ya figure?" Pete asked from behind me. We were standing at the front end of a rusted old Ford pickup truck.

"It was me, I'd probably try for the one down near the end closest to the opening of the cove."

"Makes sense, I s'ppose," he said. "Looks like the only way down is this path."

I studied the sheds below as best I could in the limited light provided by a couple of lights on a few sheds. They didn't seem to be connected in any way.

"Okay, let's go. Let's keep the light down on the ground. No point in alerting him."

We made our way along the path. We were about two houses away from our destination when Pete's light landed on the body of a dead dog chained up in the yard of the last house.

"Shit," I muttered. "Be careful."

The path ended above a shed with a small pier jutting out. There was a low-watt light on the shed that cast a pale glow over the boat tied there. It was one of those wide-beamed boats similar to those commonly used by inshore fishermen. There was a small open wheelhouse at the front end and a covered hatch taking up much of the open deck space.

I took a quick look around the area, trying to plan out our approach with the best chance of living through this and getting our man.

After a moment, I signalled to Pete to move off to my left so he could cover the other side of the boat while I took this side. Once he was in position, he waved to me.

It was time.

"Borden. This is the police. Toss your weapon on the deck and step out with your hands up," I shouted, shining my light down onto the boat.

There was no response for several moments. Then the ground a foot to my left exploded from two bullets, sending a few bits of gravel into my face. I instinctively lowered my head.

I didn't see where he was shooting from but assumed it had to be from inside the wheelhouse.

"Give it up," I yelled. "You haven't got a chance. The navy knows about you and the U-boat. You got nowhere to go."

Nothing. After a moment, I called over to Pete, "You see anything?"

"Nope. I think he's inside the wheelhouse," he called back.

All of a sudden, I heard a noise from behind me. Looking back, I saw the silhouette of a tall man holding a rifle.

"Police. Get back inside," I yelled at him, but he just stood there. I didn't want to risk exposing myself so I said, "Get the hell back inside and stay there or I'll arrest you."

The man hesitated a moment, then backed inside his house and closed the door.

"I think he's tryin' to start the motor," Pete called out at the same moment.

I turned back to the boat, chancing a quick peek over the edge; That was when I heard the unmistakable sound of a engine trying to turn over. I also noted that the boat was still tied to the pier, fore and aft.

"Jus' how ya figurin' on lettin' go your lines?" I called out. He still didn't respond.

"We don't need to do this. Give it up an' take your chances with the navy."

I heard the motor kick in.

"Pete. Cover the forward lines. I got the back one," I yelled. I shimmied over to the right to get a better bead on the pier. I suddenly spotted Borden, or a part of his upper body. I took aim and squeezed off two quick shots. Both hit the wheelhouse, one shattering a window, the other impacting part of the wooden frame. Pete also fired a single shot from his position, hitting the deck near the hatch.

"Uuugghh," I heard Borden grunt just before three rapid shots hit the ground where I had just vacated.

"Jesus Christ, man. It's over. We don't hafta do this," I yelled. He fired twice more.

All of a sudden, there was a loud bang from a weapon behind me. I automatically ducked down as I looked back. I saw the man I just ordered back inside the house silhouetted in the second floor window. He held a raised rifle out from under the window.

"I think I got the bastard," he yelled. "Try an' steal my boat."

"I think he's down," Pete called out a second later.

"You," I yelled up at him, "stay there. Pete, cover me. I'm goin' down."

"Gotcha," he said.

I inched forward and looked down below. I saw a body lying on the deck. I got my feet under me and slowly made my way down to the pier. Staying close to the side of the shed, I sidestepped to the front. Looking past the corner, I watched the boat for any movement. Nothing. I stepped out, and crouching low, moved quickly to the boat.

I heard a low moan come from the boat.

Stepping over the gunwale to the deck of the boat with my gun out in front of me, I made my way foward.

The German lay on his back moaning. His suppressed gun was on the deck several feet away. I shone my light on him. I saw the bloodstain on the right side of his chest. I also saw a hole in the sleeve of his jacket. I guessed one of my shots found a mark.

I put my gun away and bent down on a knee. Turning his face toward me, I saw that he was fading. Fast.

"It's over," I yelled up to Pete. "Go back to the car and radio in. Tell Parks his man isn't goin' to make it. Then you head back. First though, go to that house there," I said pointing, "and tell the man in the house who took the shot to get dressed and come down here. I'll get him to take me an' the body back. Tell Parks we'll land at King's Wharf."

"Okay," Pete called down.

I stood up and went to pick up the gun, then went into the wheelhouse. I found a radio set and a couple of small books. Flipping through one of them, I saw nothing but a series of numbers and letters. I guessed it was a codebook. Parks would have a field day with this.

I looked back at the man I knew as Borden and saw that he had finally given up the ghost. I stepped up next to his body and looked down.

"Shouldda given up."

EPILOGUE

One week after that night in Herring Cove, I was sitting with Lieutenant Michael Parks in the officers' mess at Stadacona. I was there at his invitation. The mess steward had just delivered two tall whisky and waters; a benefit of the officer class.

A lot happened since that night.

The corvette Parks had sent out made contact with the U-boat but lost it very quickly as it fled to the open sea. The big success was naval intelligence's getting their hands on a German radio set and a codebook, although it turned out to be ineffective since the Germans had developed a new code system. However, they did gain some insight into how the Germans constructed these things.

"Cheers," Parks said, raising his glass.

"Cheers," I repeated.

We both took a good sip. It tasted delicious. The real McCoy, an aged twelve year old Scotch. A rarity in the city outside certain preferred places.

"What's become of Kelly and O'Toole? If I can ask?" I said, taking another smaller taste.

"You can. Both have been turned over to the RCMP. They'll spend the rest of the war at an internment camp, then, all goes well for our side, they'll be repatriated to England."

"I imagine neither of them are lookin' forward to that prospect."

"Quite. In fact, Kelly was willing to negotiate a trade to avoid it."

"He's got somethin' to trade?"

"He claims to have information on the IRA's criminal activities in the US that might prove interesting to our brothers in the FBI."

"He probably does. But I'm surprised he'd be willin' to give them up."

"Dartmoor Prison is a very strong incentive, I hear," Parks said with a smile.

"Yeah. There isn't a good prison anywhere, though there are some worse than others, I suppose," I said.

He lifted his glass and took a sip, then said, "I am glad you accepted my offer for this drink. I wanted to tell you that it was a pleasure working with you and your partner. You are a very good policeman. My masters have sent a letter of gratitude to Lieutenant Morrison stating as much."

"Thanks. It was the same for us, although at first, we were a bit leery, but everything turned out okay."

"I appreciate that. It wasn't that hard to do. I like to think that I am clever enough to recognize my strengths and weaknesses, and investigating a murder was definitely one of those weaknesses."

"Yeah, well, everything worked out for the best in the end. I got to close three murder cases and you got to clean up some, uh, issues from your side"

"Here, here," he said, raising his glass again. I hope that we can work together again. I'd say we could stand another. Don't you agree?"

"Absolutely."

I would remember this day after the war. Neither of us knew that that toast would prove to be so prophetic.

But that is another story.

THE END

THANK YOU FOR READING

Did you enjoy this book?

We invite you to leave a review at the website of your choice, such as Goodreads, Amazon, Barnes & Noble, etc.

DID YOU KNOW THAT LEAVING A REVIEW...

- Helps other readers find books they may enjoy.
- Gives you a chance to let your voice be heard.
- Gives authors recognition for their hard work.
- Doesn't have to be long. A sentence or two about why you liked the book will do.

ABOUT THE AUTHOR

H. Paul Doucette has lived and worked in many countries throughout a varied career in International Transportation. He enjoyed a short career as a fine art photographer with modest success. Now retired and an avid reader of detective fiction and mystery novels, he has decided to pursue a new career as a writer. He has written two series, the first is a private detective named Matt Murphy set in Greenwich Village of the 1960s and second, the Red Sun Series, is set during the Second World war in the Pacific and follows the missions of Paul Jarvis, agent with the Counter Intelligence Corps. He lives in Nova Scotia, Canada.

ALSO BY H. PAUL DOUCETTE

WITH MELANGE BOOKS

Matt Murphy Mysteries

A Role to Kill For

Out for Blood

Silk Slippers and Tutus

Revenge is a Dish Best Served

Never Forget, Never Forgive

Dead Man in the Harbour

Red Sun Series

Red Sun Over Panama

Red Sun Over Mexico

Lightning Source UK Ltd.
Milton Keynes UK
UKHW03f2052190318
319713UK00001B/75/P